I0694784

LETTERS ON THE PARK BENCH

DIRCO DE CORSO

Published by Dirco de Corso 2015

***

***

***

***

***

ISBN 978-3-9524565-0-7

For the liberation of myself.

JOINING THE DOTS – FROM RIGHT TO LEFT

As with anything that seems counter-intuitive at first glance, taking a different approach to something that we have been used to for our entire lives may lead to unexpected insights.

I am extremely grateful for this chance at this point in my life and I would like to thank my primary school, secondary school and college teachers for their encouraging grading of my essays, even though some of them complained about the legibility of my handwriting. I want to show my gratitude to some particular teachers who cultivated a philosophical state of mind through their vivid discussions of literature, even though, despite their recommendations, I chose not to study philosophy.

Without my friends, with whom I have exchanged thousands of letters, though in bits and bytes over the years, I would not have been able to capture in words what is in your bare hands now. A seemingly silly New Year's resolution for myself when I was confident enough to say, 'one day I will write a book'.

Thanks to my work colleagues in different corporations and countries who praised me for my well-phrased correspondence of complex facts and the right words at the right time.

Finally, thanks to an almost unknown man whom I barely spoke to during an eye-opening encounter in Barcelona who asked just one question and ignited energies which empowered me to pursue what I felt just a few months earlier.

Last but not least, thanks to my parents who allowed me to discover the world. Now, reading from left to right, determining the chronological order of the above encounters it would have been hard to join the dots. Only by taking the liberty to change the perspective, pace or direction we may spot the pattern or fine line connecting the dots. I encourage you to do that with the stories that are ahead of you. Enjoy!

In the middle of somewhere,
September 2015.

III

Tim felt awkward among all the adults sat in a circle below the tree. It seemed like they had met before, yet they were unknown to each other. There were eight of them sitting cross-legged in comfortable luscious grass and soft moss which was as good as a well-padded cushion. Since there were eight of them they couldn't fit on the bench, which was beautifully located where the surface roots merged into the tree trunk. The jade coloured foliage made of countless bi-lobed fan shaped leaves was astonishing and just provided enough light and shade so that the group felt comfortable.

Though vast land surrounded the tree, Tim felt that they were in the centre of a sizeable transparent dome. They could see the outer world, they could even hear some of its noise, yet there was a calming quietness, which filled the dome unless there were some agitated discussions among the members of the group or a storm came thundering through. The larger stones in the nearby riverbed created the comforting sound of flowing water and birds were twittering the news of the day.

It was curious Cassiopeia who first recognized the pile of neatly folded papers, which were stuck into an envelope almost one inch thick. It was placed on the edge of the bench and on its front it carried no specific addressee but rather a handwritten phrase expressing a certain firmness of character and read 'To the universe'. The moment Cassiopeia wanted to grab the envelope; different opinions about their content sparked a discussion in the group. Who placed the envelope there? What did it contain? Letters? Or just blank pieces of paper?

AUTUMN

An Inseparable Pair

Mana had been looking forward to this for the whole week. She just saw it by coincidence the other day when she passed the temple for her daily prayers. She recognized a beautifully yet simply crafted poster on the noticeboard informing her of a tea master who was in town to share his valuable knowledge about the fine art of a tea ceremony.

Here she was, sitting in the lotus position with other fellow tea enthusiasts surrounded by the dark brown temple wood, the fading green of the grass in the temple's courtyard and the misty air as autumn was approaching. It was Sunday morning and Mana had arrived at the temple just after enjoying a hot noodle soup on her way here. Sitting on the wooden temple floor, waiting for the ceremony to start, she could feel her energy flowing and her curiosity rising. Closing her eyes, she instantly imagined the lush green of the tea leaves up in the hilly areas of her homeland which were covered with the emerald coloured plants. The journey of the fine art started with the fresh leaves being carefully plucked by the hands of tea farmers, which had been doing so for generations. Drops of water ran off the leaves as they ended up in the basket before being carefully dried and processed. What a journey it must have been for the leaves before they ended up in our teacup.

Back in the real world, Mana was watching the tea master serenely starting his preparations, leaving her with the impression that he had a deeply rooted passion and his sole purpose and at the same time his destiny on planet Earth was to introduce people to the secrets of the emerald gold. The sound of the water, which started boiling slowly, was the only thing Mana recognized besides the few words spoken by the taciturn master. Everyone respected the tranquillity surrounding the moment while paying utmost attention to the smooth movements of the master guiding them through the steps. He appeared to move his limbs without any strength and in a completely harmonious flow, with only his breath in the slightly chilly autumn breeze a visible sign of his effort. As steam was making its presence known and the water was ready, tiny glass cups were arranged. The selected fine remains of the tea leaves were waiting in the glass pot for the water to be poured. The moment the master started pouring the water into the pot, the tiny leaves started moving like swimmers in a synchronized swimming performance, random at first glance but then dancing perfectly in sync upon closer inspection.

Holding a cup of tea in her hand, grateful for what she was witnessing, Mana closed her eyes again to feel the warmth deep inside her as she took small sips of the tea. Off went her mind, following the journey of the tea leaves that travelled the world before people could enjoy the result of the beautiful symbiosis of tea and water.

RIVER OF LIFE

Cassiopeia was in a philosophical mood today. Sitting at the shore of the small river near her home she was observing the flow of the water. It appeared to her that much of the water's ecosphere could be compared with a human's life. When born we are pure and unbiased like a stone thrown into the river's source. Still sharp and a little rough, the stone starts its journey from spring to sea. As Cassiopeia sat there, her thoughts were bubbling continuously and she found that many facets of the river resembled a human's life.

As we are born and slowly grow up, many things influence us. So does the water with the stone, as it is moved forward down the riverbed by the current of the water. During the journey the stones might go through unnatural riverbeds, which were created to make room for the rural expansion of human beings. Like humans at school, in those parts of the regulated river, the stones follow a more or less given path with less chance of following other river branches. Though the stones might come out a little less sharp thereafter, they are still all inherently different in shape, colour and consistency.

As life goes on, the stones in the river will be moulded in the different environments of the river. Melting water, which increases the level of the river, would flush some of them quickly to other parts. Others might get stuck when water levels are low and the riverbed has nearly dried up. So, some stones will end up less or more refined than others sooner.

While picturing the riverbed, Cassiopeia imagined being a water drop in the riverbed. It could easily move around obstacles and avoid being stuck. This is not so for the stones, as they face many awkward situations. If a small stone is blocked by a big rock in the middle of the river, how could the small stone ever move forward? It would be subject to the force of the water yet it could hardly find a way out of the situation. That appeared to Cassiopeia to be a perfect description of what a modern slave in the capitalist world would face. Being taken hostage by their dissatisfaction at work while having to cope with their daily business and personal obligations. Changing this desperate situation into a promising opportunity might not only be in the hands of those affected, but like the stone in the riverbed, would also depend on the next unexpected rise of the water levels. Therefore, the seemingly big obstacle in the way would become irrelevant as the current of the water would move the small stone back to an open path. So water can be of great help for the onward journey of the stones. But with its continuous force, which rarely seems to vanish, the water is to the stone what the buzz of the world in the 21st century is to humans. Taking a breath to reflect where to step next, one could easily be washed away. Absorbed in professional and private daily matters, one would have to be a very heavy stone to remain still in the water.

Whether water is around or not, the path of the stones seemed to be determined more by chance than by deliberate choice. While stones might be part of a group as they make their journey towards the sea, travelling alongside each other, stones might part or regroup as the riverbed evolves from a narrow rivulet to a wide wild stream. Much like human relationships, some stones seemed to move forward at a similar pace, while others are set apart by the sudden surges of water.

Cassiopeia wondered whether stones could produce offspring like humans do. Maybe, when the stones hit other and the impact makes them split into multiple parts. A new phase would start, as the previously rounded off stones suddenly become sharp again. Like fresh parents with a new-born, it would take time to get accustomed to the new path of life.

Distracted by people walking past, Cassiopeia's thoughts paused for a while before she recalled a discussion she had had with her friends the other day. Growing up they liked to pursue odd ideas in order to differentiate themselves. How would that be reflected in her philosophical excursus of water and stones? Would stones that remained in one location be considered as going against the stream? Against the unforeseeable path set out by destiny? While remaining in the same place in the riverbed, would the stones' edges be rounded off as they would during the journey downstream? Who assumed that the round shape of a stone is the ideal shape one could strive for? Being moulded by a location's environment might reveal unexpected enclosures in a stone's structure like the undiscovered talents of her friends.

How does it end after all? Getting smaller and smaller, with not much left but hopefully the inner core, satisfaction and the wisdom that life is a unique gift,

Cassiopeia pictured that the stones would be washed into the salty sea as tiny sand grains.

As the day was coming to an end, it was time for Cassiopeia to head home. Recently she had started studying Journalism and Russian. It was not to her liking really because she felt that in today's world only certifications count, not deeply rooted motivation. But in any case, she had to prepare for her lecture tomorrow.

'The freedom pass'

It was early Monday morning and Marc was sitting at the boarding gate. As usual he was returning to his project before the day dawned and the week really started. He had had an awful weekend and quarrelled badly with Laura for the first time in many years. He couldn't even recall the reason for the quarrel, nor could he remember the chain of arguments that followed from both sides. It dawned on Marc that most likely the issue wasn't with Laura at all but rather his current disorientation, exhaustion and unhappiness. But again, as with all the other things bothering him, he wasn't at all quite sure.

He was waiting for his turn to board. Deeply absorbed in his own thoughts, he felt cushioned from the hectic world as if he were in a dream bubble. For the first time in a long time, flying off on Monday morning wasn't a pain, but a pleasure. After so many years in this profession, Marc usually felt like all the other consultants who made their way to their clients on a weekly basis – exhausted and bored of flying. Marc could easily associate himself with all the travellers that felt anxious about their air travel because of the unusual sensation flying would bring with it. However, he rarely found himself as excited as children, who were off on their holidays and who were travelling on an aircraft for the first time. But today he was maybe not excited but certainly relieved.

Suddenly, the omnipresent possibility to escape the worries in his daily life with the option of flying off seemed like a pass to freedom. The boarding pass, embodying the apparent freedom, turned into an entitlement to escape from facing and solving the challenges presented to us.

Barely noting the announcements, Marc heard the final call for all remaining passengers.

POTPOURRI OF SCENTS

How exciting! Today Tim's classes were going to take place outdoors, in the forest near the school. Though already a little chilly these days, the weather forecast promised a sunny day with blue skies. Anyway, Tim needn't have worried as his mum made sure his clothes were warm enough.

Having gathered in the school playground, Tim and his classmates followed their science and biology teachers to the forest. As they were approaching it, an increasing number of leaves lined their path. Tim enjoyed walking through all the leaves that were covering the ground like a collage of different pieces of coloured paper. He particularly enjoyed the rustling of the leaves depending on their dryness and would have loved walking back and forth to discover the different degrees of rustling.

As his course mates headed on, Tim took a short break from walking. He was busy figuring out the mixture of scents in the air. While all the colours of autumn easily divert our attention, Tim's nose was trying to distinguish the crisp and clean smell of the chilly autumn air, the sweetness of conifer resin and the herby, nutty scents emanating from the drying leaves covering the ground.

Stopping at an acorn tree, Tim figured that even the squirrels seemed to be busy preparing for the change of season as he caught many of them collecting acorns. Pausing to watch the squirrels that were busy stocking up for winter, Tim realized how many acorns were among the leaves on the ground. Shiny and sometimes hidden like pearls in their shells, Tim tried to pick up some intact acorns from the ground. Despite his teachers calling him, Tim picked up another one and started assessing it from all sides. With all the different colours of brown striped on the long side, this oval shape looked like a Zeppelin to Tim. Caught in his own imagination, Tim almost forgot that it was close to lunchtime and he was supposed to help his classmates with preparing the fire in order to barbeque their meat and vegetables. Though a little difficult due the humid ground, together with the teachers they were able to light the fire. Barely 20 minutes later Tim's nose was filled with the smell of burning wood, a sign that the embers were ready for their sausages to be grilled. The smell of the barbeque intensified as the raw meat hit the fire. Hardly paying attention to his lunch in the making, Tim was busy looking around. Many large trees surrounded the fire. Just enough to limit the wind but plenty of room for the sun to shed some light and provide his friends with some warmth. The trees must have been around for ages. Just before lunch the teachers were explaining how to count the age of a tree. Tim was amazed by the information one could gather when looking at the annual rings of a tree. It seemed that firm and long-lasting things needed time to grow. Tim? Your sausage is ready!

NATURE'S ORCHESTRA

Marc didn't look happy today; wearing his yellow raincoat over his impeccable designer suit he was enjoying the rain this autumn evening. He was watching the stones change colour as the raindrops hit each of them.

Recently things had been tough for Marc. Away from home working on his project, he often came to sit here. The project he was currently working on didn't seem to be going as planned and as project manager he was being blamed for it. Pressure had been mounting over the last few weeks. Things at home weren't good either, as his long-term girlfriend Laura had started to distance herself ever since Marc had started working as a consultant a year ago. She was such a lovely girl, caring for him as much as she could to give him a good start in this new job. But Marc, exhausted from his weeks on the road, just spent his days at home sleeping, trying to recover from the long working days. Being constantly connected with his work in a wireless world, he felt tense. Like a personal dictator in his pocket, he caught himself checking his smartphone as soon as he opened his eyes in the morning, while getting ready in the bathroom, while pretending to enjoy his whole-wheat cereal with fruit from the breakfast buffet, on the road, while getting a cup of coffee from the coffee dispenser, while swallowing his Subway sandwich during lunch….even when he was off work, and was spending time with Laura, his mind was wandering. His hand reaching into his pocket, to just check whether he had missed a call, received a new email or forgotten about an appointment…

It was during these moments of time on his own after work but away from home when Marc felt his chest getting tight and he needed to escape the seemingly peaceful and comfortable environment of the five star hotel where he spent most of his time unless he was with a client or at home for the weekend. Listening to the rain somehow made him feel relieved. As the rain intensified Marc seemed to be absorbed in his thoughts while the raindrops hit the leaves, the wood, the branches, the pebbles, the nearby rubbish bin, the lake in front and the street lamp next to him started to sound like an orchestra beginning its first piece. Perfectly in sync, without a conductor, nature seemed to be performing an outstanding musical piece, capturing Marc's mood with its fundamental melancholic tones.

SHADES OF GREY

Sleepy from the boring classes in the morning and her stomach full with lunch draining all the oxygenized blood from her brain, Cassiopeia took a nap on a bench near the edge of the campus below a tree. Nearly all the leaves were gone. The remaining autumn sun was warming Cassiopeia's chin, cheek, part of her nose and temple.

As soon as Cassiopeia had got used to the hardness of the bench her mind started to wander. In her short siesta she dreamt of an odd day. A day full of shades of grey. A day where someone just seemed to have forgotten to switch on the light. With no sun, everything seemed dull. The usually brightly coloured flowers didn't even catch the attention of a single tourist who would pause to admire nature's beauty in the best daylight. Stunning lakes wouldn't appear to be steel blue, reflecting the clouds like floating pieces of cotton wool on the water. Even if there was snow, with the fascinating glittering of the crystals missing, the magic of the pure white would be gone. Sun worshippers would be walking aimlessly around the beach while looking for something to warm their bodies.

How grateful she was as she woke from her dream and realized that the sun was still warming her face. It felt like it was burning already as the surrounding temperature was a little chilly. How dull life would be if the sun didn't rise day after day to turn our surroundings into a kaleidoscope of colours.

Reason for longing

Mana was on her way home. She wanted to stop at her favourite bench in the park again before passing by the temple to say her daily prayers. But the weather seemed to be at odds with her plan. The park was already deserted as everybody had gone home because the sky was darkening and big heavy raindrops were forcing their way from the sky to the ground. It was the end of autumn and winter was just around the corner. The strong wind, which caused the trees in the park to bend in random directions, couldn't dissuade Mana from her way.

Mana didn't particularly like autumn. With the summer gone, she always felt the cold, grey, wet autumn weather made people feel lonely. Her heart was longing for warmth. Longing for a hug or a warm hand to hold her cold one. Longing for someone to wake her up gently in the morning as she was left with no choice then but to leave her warm and cosy bed in order to find her way through the cold to the office. Now that she was nearly home she wished someone would caress her while she was sitting on her couch watching her favourite TV series. Where is the one who would kiss her goodnight before she went off to her dreams?

It's all a matter of perspective

If Walter had learnt one thing during his 76 years of life, it was that perspective really matters. He was reminded again and again as he was sitting next to Ruth on the bench in the park whenever they went for a walk like they were doing today. Ruth was at least a foot shorter than Walter and thus her view of the world was already different from his. A foot seems like a small difference but when it comes to how we view the world it could make a big difference. While he was really fed up with Ruth's obsession about astrological reasoning for everything that happened in the world, he always tried to see the world through her eyes, which were about a foot lower than his.

He wished people would open their eyes every day as if it were their first day of life seeing this strange world for the first time, from a new perspective, never being tired of being curious and grateful for the new day ahead.

BUBBLES

It was a little rough outside today, the wind had been blowing in all directions, but fortunately for Cassiopeia it hadn't rained yet and she could spend her break outside. Recalling her outing in town with friends after class yesterday, she thought about the observations she had made.

In a hectic connected world that never sleeps we are trapped by marketing bubbles making us want to believe that we will enjoy a moment of peace while sipping a branded and overpriced cup of coffee, chewing a vitamin loaded sandwich made entirely of organic produce or indulging in a rejuvenating power massage which is a contradiction in itself.

We try to escape the constant buzz of the civilized world by resorting to artificial bubbles which promise temporary relief. But once the paper cup of coffee is empty, the last bite of the sandwich has been swallowed and the time slot of the massage has ended, we are back in the endless rat race without realizing that bubbles burst without warning and did not provide us with the islands of serenity that we long for. Even though the bubbles were blown away and reshuffled from time to time when a new hype emerged which promised more, better or quicker escapes, satisfaction didn't settle in. Rather, with marketing experts creating more and more sophisticated bubbles for which we were willing to pay an increasing amount of money, our pockets are emptied quicker and the search for peace continues.

CLOSE TO ICU

Driven by power-plays, conflicting personal and political interests, Marc wondered which of his clients would survive the next 10 years even though they have been around for a long time. To Marc companies appeared to be like battery powered robots, whereby the batteries were equal to human beings. But these batteries had a big disadvantage; they needed to be replaced more often these days as they ran down quicker and quicker. But Marc's perception was that companies didn't really bother that exchanging batteries is costly in the long run. They continued to firmly believe that the robot would function as expected anyway, regardless of the condition of the batteries, even though an attentive technician would have had to admit that the robot was in such a dysfunctional operational state that it would have had to be admitted to hospital if it were a human being.

But all that mattered was that the robots had to be painted in the brightest colour available every year to deceive the onlookers and owners of the robots about the outdated and unsustainable modus operandi beyond the shiny and polished surface. One would expect that as robots become more sophisticated, they would develop some self-learning capabilities. However, rather the opposite was true; the mechanics seemed to malfunction repeatedly at the same points.

With robots being specialized and just covering one part of many sequences of work, the batteries are being plugged in, moved as required or even discarded to the liking of the robot strategists. Disregarding any possible consequence for the involved batteries that draw at least part of their energy from the fruits of their labour and the recognition they receive for it. This was not really an appealing outlook Marc found.

CAUGHT BY IMAGINATION

Today's science class was interesting. For the first time Tim heard about the different attempts of humans wanting to fly and all the apparatus they built in order to take to the skies. What struck Tim was that many of the flying objects looked very much like birds. He wondered how humans would have shaped what they call aircraft today if they weren't following the shape of a bird.
We can create something entirely new from our thoughts but for inspiration we often turn to nature. Nevertheless, without leaving an opportunity to be caught by imagination, the world would be a dull place to live.

OVERFLOWING SPONGE

Eyes wide open, her mind far from resting, Mana was completely awake instead of feeling sleepy though it was already close to midnight. It was dark and peacefully quiet in her room yet she felt like torrential rain was hitting her skin all over her body. Mana was stunned by all her impressions of the day. Nothing in particular had happened; it was just like any other working day. But with stimuli all over the place her senses had been completely busy for most of the day.

She had been standing in the cramped subway with human noise all around her and a constant buzz of mobile devices. Flashing electronic billboards praised the newest anti-aging formulas and advertisements of the latest limited edition lip gloss, which was supposed to do wonders upon its application. The heated discussions of the neighbouring table during lunchtime were about a husband committing adultery. The latest gossip in the office about who dislikes who, what was being done wrong or right in projects. The music of the teenager next to her on her way home who was blasting his ears with some strong beats, disregarding the health of his eardrums. The noise of the cars forming an endless parade of metal as they were stuck in a traffic jam as Mana walked home from the station to her apartment. And so on, and so on.

And this was just what Mana was aware of, but there was much more. All the stuff that we perceived unconsciously, where our conscious brain was just being fed, if at all, the headlines of what was happening, compared to the complete unconscious story, which remains beyond our reach. Absorbing all the information gathered by our senses like a sponge, it isn't surprising that at one point we will run into a memory overflow which leaves us restless at night.

Much of our energy in today's hectic world seems to be used to digest as many impressions as possible unless we deliberately pause, leave space for our mind, conscious and unconscious to work on what it has perceived, not just during sleep but also during the day.

Determined to avoid insomnia, Mana felt it was time to revive her daily meditation habit of creating a quiet room for personal reflection regardless of her busy schedule.

THREADS OF LIFE

With the air getting a little chillier as Cassiopeia was watching the river near her house she was glad she was wearing her wool jumper, which her grandmother had knitted for her some years ago. Even though a little out of fashion, it felt comfortable and for Cassiopeia the craft itself was an excellent metaphor for how things are made up of more than just the sum of their parts.

Cassiopeia held the firm belief that upon birth every one of us is given a tin full of threads of life. With those threads we mark the paths we take or intend to take on our journey. Unlike the threads of amino acids following the strict laws of nature, forming our DNA which can be found in all parts of us, the tin of the threads of life is more like a personal ball of wool which doesn't seem to follow any pattern or abide by any law.

In order to determine what the future holds for us we might easily be tempted to quickly empty the contents of the tin onto a drawing board in an attempt to find out what surprises the threads reveal and how all of them fit together.

But we rarely have the chance to go against our destiny, rather, with all of the threads having two different ends and some of the threads being short, some long, some of intense colours, some faded, some straight and others curled up we were puzzled though hopefully not discouraged but definitely challenged by the seemingly unlimited number of possibilities for combining them.

Emptying the whole tin in one go was not an option so we ended up pulling, consciously or unconsciously, one thread out of the dark interior of the tin. Without having a glimpse inside and with a certain uncertainty we decided on the next thread that we would add to our journey. Once in our hands some of us appear determined and follow a clear picture in our minds for how to arrange the threads best to get all the way to where we want to be, while others take a zigzag path which they find suits them better. At times unable to hold all the reins together we might lose a thread as we progress, but somehow, as with the secret and inaccessible laws of nature, we eventually reach a point where the missing piece is suddenly complemented by another thread which previously seemed unsuitable. As unique as all the individuals were, equally as unique were the sequences of threads that all of us produced, with none of them being the best but all of them deserving respect and all of them creating something more admirable than just a ball of wool.

CROSSROADS AND DEAD-ENDS

Marc couldn't get a single thing done the whole day. Totally discouraged, he was sitting in the park again willing the fresh air to clear his mind. As the world seemed to close in on him he felt like a train off the tracks. Driving full force in the seemingly right direction until a sudden incident turns everything upside down. But there wasn't a specific incident that had tipped Marc off the track. It was the accumulation of everything happening around him that made him feel exhausted, tired and lost.

The never-ending pressure from all the projects at work often left him restless when he tried to get a good sleep at night. He had started to question himself about why he was so eager to be a consultant, what contribution would he make to the world except for the concepts and slides that he was highly paid for? Sure, he helped his clients in some way, but was the remuneration worth all the pain?

And now that Laura had suddenly asked him whether they should take a break, what should he live for?

It seemed to him that life was like a lengthy dinner with an uncountable number of dishes skilfully prepared by someone for the guest to enjoy. But right now his life didn't have that excitement of trying a new dish again and again; it was like eating all the apparently delicious dishes without being able to distinguish the taste of all the flavours. If someone were to ask him which of the dishes he liked most, he wouldn't be able to tell them. At the same time he was bored and somehow exhausted by being required to make decisions day-by-day, hour-by-hour. But he also knew that if he couldn't make his stand clear towards Laura, their paths would part, at least for now, and that seemed like a lot at stake.

The sun was about to set and it became chillier. Though he still had Laura, Marc felt like there wasn't much to look forward to in his life. Whichever junction he approached, whichever decision he made, he always felt the outcome was wrong or different from his expectations. He either ended up at the next junction or at a dead-end, in both cases with only one option – to decide where to go next.

It seemed like he had lost the vision that had been driving him all the way forward until this point in time. Like holding a map of his life upside down, the vision blurred by fog, he couldn't figure out where to place his feet next. How he wished the night would be clear today and the moon would illuminate the undiscovered paths on his map of life.

As Marc was about to leave the park a monk in his orange coloured cowl asked his permission to sit next to him. The omnipresent smile on the monk's face, which seemed to stem from deeply rooted satisfaction and gratefulness, irritated Marc initially. However, after glancing at each other briefly a few times, the unconditional happiness somehow had a calming effect on Marc's current state. Hesitating at first, the dissimilar pair started to engage in a conversation. The friendly stranger did not speak much, as if his tongue was made of gold, yet his attentive facial expression made Marc feel understood. It was unusual for Marc to reveal much of his struggles to anyone, but in the course of this unexpected encounter it just came naturally.

Occasional nods from the monk encouraged Marc to continue, though tiredness started to settle in and his phrases became more and more fragmented and disorderly. Unsurprisingly it didn't escape the monk's attentiveness.

When parting the monk concluded the conversation by encouraging Marc to deliberately observe positive encounters of all kinds. Instead of looking for missing paths he should cultivate his curiosity, which would help him to identify open doors. Then he rose and left the park, walking across a bridge over a small river in the centre of the park. Bridges, Marc thought. Look for bridges.

BEGRUDGED ATTENTION

Ruth was on her way to town to meet her friend Esther. As Walter was also out she decided to take the bus, which she rarely did. It was completely crowded with kids and a few mothers with babies. Out of courtesy, one of the mothers offered her seat to Ruth and stood up instead of sitting down. Only when Ruth wanted to thank her for her politeness did she realize that the young mum had earphones plugged into her ears and was starring at her smartphone, not realizing that someone had just thanked her for her courteous behaviour. Never mind, Ruth thought, until she realized that the adorable baby in the stroller was also looking for her mum's attention. She was even mumbling at her but did not get any response.
Ruth felt anger and disappointment rising in her. Some silly stuff which the child's mum was moving around with her thumb on a screen was actually more important than giving her attention to her daughter seated in front of her! How could it possibly be that affection towards the growing generation in a modern world is being compromised by our unconscious

addiction to so-called smart devices? They don't seem to make us any smarter in our human interactions. How could we possibly surrender to technology without having doubts in our mind about how our children will develop a solid set of social values, listening skills and the ability to lead discussions face-to-face if their parents are not their examples? Ruth was lost for words.

OUTPACING PATIENCE

Cassiopeia was frustrated with her progress in learning Russian. Her results hadn't shown any improvement for months despite her hard work. Was she just not patient enough or did she lack the necessary talent for languages? Curled up on her couch at home, she started pondering about patience. Why was it that we can be generously patient with everyone except ourselves? Is it because of our expectations? Is it due to the expectations of the meritocratic society surrounding us, which makes us believe that all our achievements need to be valued, assessed and compared with others? Or does it originate from within ourselves because we lack the confidence that everything will turn out well despite our inherent adversity to uncertainty? Because we always want to know what the future holds for us? Has the increased pace in our daily lives led to an inquisitive state of mind which means we always want to know what is next? Or is it just our curiosity? Is being impatient a flaw or a gift of evolution? I bet it's a gift. So, slow down Cassiopeia and pause. Pleasant surprises rarely come in the spur of the moment.

Eyes on You

Mana was out on a rare shopping trip for winter clothes. It was not something that she liked doing because she felt timid and her lack of self-confidence always overcame her when she had to bear the eyes of the sales personnel the moment she stepped out from the changing room. Direct questions intimidated her and all the people looking around randomly in the shops made her feel like an alien. But why was that? She never felt inappropriate in her job. Was it because the private Mana was afraid to be who she really is?

TWO SIDES OF THE COIN

Enrique was tired. Despite the odds of the weather he decided to have his lunch in the man-made park between the airport terminals before flying off to his meeting just after noon.

He felt disturbed and weary as he had heard some heart-breaking noises coming from his neighbour above him last night. It was the first time he had heard such haunting noises in his own apartment.

He was used to many odd situations and noises in hotels wherever he travelled. Though hotel walls often softened the source of the noise, his curiosity and attentiveness usually prevented him from sleeping as his mind kept him awake trying to figure out whether he was witnessing a serious argument between friends who were close to killing each other or whether he was embarrassed because the joys enjoyed by a young couple made him blush even while he was trying to sleep. But Enrique never felt affected or somehow that he needed to intervene while facing such incidents with his temporary neighbours during his travels. The only thing he usually tried to do, again out of curiosity, was to figure out what his neighbours looked like while he was getting himself breakfast at the buffet the following day. Could it be those two guests sitting next to him on the left? Or the sleepy but happy couple entering the breakfast area shortly before the service stopped?

Anyway, it didn't matter right now. Enrique felt uncomfortable because suddenly he realized that being connected and in touch with all his friends all over the world, he knew much more about what his friend Mel in Singapore was experiencing or what had happened to Paul the other day in Sydney as he nearly got run over by a car, but he knew close to nothing about the people surrounding him in what he called home.

The only thing he knew about the neighbour above him was that she was a single mother who had just given birth a few months ago. He didn't even know what she looked like or why she had ended up being a single mum just after giving birth.

What he had heard was still vividly present in his mind as he was trying to imagine possible reasons for the sobbing and crying he had heard last night. It was clearly an adult's noise but what could have possibly happened? Was there something wrong with the new-born? Had the mother fallen ill? Was she heartbroken so she could no longer care for her baby?

Enrique felt bad speculating about the possible reasons. Should he have just gone up and knocked on the door? He should have done that, certainly.

He decided to ask his direct neighbour, a nice grandmotherly lady living on the same floor as him about what he had heard last night when he was back tomorrow morning.

REACHING FOR THE SKY

Tim had had an exhausting day. It wasn't the normal gym class but a mini triathlon that his sports teacher had organized. Tim had just got back home and was lying on the bench in his parents' garden, and a moment later he was off into a deep sleep. He enjoyed this kind of sleep, as his mind would always take him somewhere interesting. It felt like sitting in the driver's seat of his dad's car. The night was dark and a little fresh, but inside the cosy car, Tim barely heard anything except for the music coming from the radio. As he accelerated the road markings seemed to pass by quicker and quicker…he soon entered a tunnel where lights at the left and right hand side of the road appeared to be flashing as he travelled with his imaginary vehicle. No one was on the road except for him; the world seemed to be at peace while it was asleep. Cruising aimlessly, Tim sat in the driver's seat, fully absorbed in his own thoughts while attentively observing what was happening around him. It was a clear autumn night, not many animals were out there, yet a few insects hit the windscreen as Tim was moving along in his bubble. Shortly before they hit the car, the insects seemed to appear in the car's spotlights, screaming while realizing their destiny. Yet Tim couldn't hear anything. The car seemed to lose contact with the road and the lights flew pass. Tim felt like he was taking off.

As the lights went off and the world came to a standstill, Tim caught sight of some cats on the side of the road. They seemed to be enjoying the remaining warmth of the tarmac while observing what this odd human being was doing at this hour. Tim wasn't alone in the airspace, birds flying steadily over the middle lands crossed his route and headed towards the golden orange coloured pie in the middle of the sky. Slowing down, Tim passed by one of the few houses where the lights were still on. Peaking briefly into the window while stepping off the accelerator, Tim saw a couple gesticulating heavily while facing each other. Time to speed up again. Tim was aiming for the stars, twinkling like tiny diamonds on dark blue velvet, their gravity was inescapable.

What? Ah, it was just a dream. One of those that Tim enjoyed, but now his mum was calling him to come for dinner.

PERFECTLY IRRATIONAL

Marc just needed to get out. Even though it meant he could only sit peacefully in his favourite spot in the park for a few minutes, he desperately needed a few breaths of fresh air. For the past few days he had been involved in some heated discussions with his client on how to accelerate the project they were currently working on. Speed was essential again, and so was money spent on expensive consultants. Marc was used to sudden changes in plans, especially when new management came on board. Usually the urge for recognition kicks in with these new managers as they try to shape the organisation to their liking. Which can be fine because fresh ideas certainly bring value to organisations, which have been ticking like clockwork for many years without any consideration of change.

However, Marc's frustration was rooted somewhere else. In all the meetings with senior managers, of both his client as was well as from his firm, the discussions were unstructured most of the time. In the absence of any clear goal or objective and with an ever-changing group of participants in the workshops over the last few weeks, deadlines had been postponed, outcomes of previous discussions were questioned repeatedly and the initial intention of acceleration was brushed aside by political battles. What upset Marc most was not the endless wasted hours of preparation and discussions, though that had certainly contributed to his volatile mood, but that a group of apparently senior leaders with a wealth of experience were marking time instead of progressing, and the main cause could clearly be attributed to their non-negotiable personal and purely egoistic goals. While those goals might have seemed perfectly rational to the individual, the collective sum of all the egoistic actions became perfectly irrational. And the frightening part was that none of the involved managers seemed to take note of it, or rather intentionally ignored it because any other outcome might have jeopardized their own goals. Marc started to wonder whether he was suitable for such kinds of corporate battles in the long run or whether he might opt for a withdrawal from such a battlefield, because besides frustration, collateral damage to satisfaction, happiness and eventually health seemed to be disproportionately high.

A WORLD OF DISTRACTIONS

It was a rather rare occasion that Enrique was in the office for a few days in a row. But this week there weren't many activities planned. Usually Enrique would pack some lunch from his favourite bocadillo shop around the corner and eat it at his desk. But ever since being in the office yesterday he felt a little restless, or to be more precise rather distracted. Though it was a little chilly, he hoped to take his mind off things by enjoying his lunch in the Parc de la Ciutadella.

When he got to the office yesterday his colleagues shared some rumours that they had heard the other week. It seemed that the executive board was talking about initiating a reorganization, which would potentially also concern Enrique's department. Though this jeopardized Enrique's concentration, it wasn't the only cause affecting his ability to focus on his work. As many times before, it was a female of the human species that was distracting him.

Chewing his chorizo-filled barra de pan, Enrique's mind recollected flashes of memories from the day before. While he had heard that a new human resource colleague had joined about a month ago, he had never met her in person as he was always out of the office travelling to his customers. But yesterday he had been introduced to Luz, a tall and stunning looking human resource consultant in her early thirties. What struck Enrique was her confident appearance as well as her charming smile and shoulder-length blonde curly hair. She just dropped by Enrique's desk during the day yesterday to introduce herself. Which would have been alright, but she returned to the very same place in a chatty mood before leaving the office. While Enrique was trying to finish his monthly reports for his boss, Luz leant against Enrique's desk. Recalling the scene, Enrique still felt odd. At first he pulled back his chair, leant backwards into a relaxed pose and continued to chat to Luz. Her being almost as tall as him, Enrique suddenly felt unsure about which pose to take. When Luz started saying he shouldn't worry about the rumours he'd heard because he is known for his outstanding performance and she would 'take care of him', Enrique was confused. Luckily it was winter and Luz was already wearing her coat, ready to leave the office. If it had been summer Enrique was sure he wouldn't have been able to take his eyes off her and she might have caught him blatantly starring at her.

Lunchtime was nearly over. Unfortunately, the chilly air and change of environment hadn't really improved Enrique's state of mind but he didn't have a choice but to go back to the office to get his work done.

NATURE'S PROTÉGÉ

Exhausted from everything his six senses had perceived during the busy day, Tim fell asleep the moment he hit his comfortable bed. Taking his favourite pre-natal foetal sleeping position, he imagined lying on a giant bed of luscious green moss. Its surface seemed to be made of tiny brushes, which were as soft as ripe cotton buds. It adapted well to Tim's body and his sleeping position and made him feel safe. Autumn was around the corner and the air was filled with a tangy smell emitted by the ground, which was exhausted from all the growth throughout spring and summer. Now it needed a break to recuperate. When Tim was on his way home today he watched the bumblebees bouncing off the lavender stalks. The comparably big yet still tiny bumblebees seemed to enjoy landing and talking off from the shaky stalks which were becoming weaker. Another cone-shaped flower, which had its yellow ray florets pointing out and down, appeared to Tim like a rocket ready to be dispatched, containing seeds for the next generation of flowers in the year to come. Birds were collecting the last sunflower seeds from the sunflower heads, which had an amazing spiral pattern.

But now, Tim was half awake, half asleep on his imaginary bed of moss below an old oak tree. Though rain was approaching from afar, Tim felt safe and sound and his nostrils captured the first breath of clean air as the rain started to hit the soil. Drop by drop the refreshing and soothing breeze surrounded him. With it was the onset of a concert of a million drummers slowly beating their tiny drums, not fully clear but slightly softened and rather deep in tone as all the raindrops hit the ground around him. Tim didn't get wet. His imaginary strongly rooted oak tree with its solid roots just above the ground ensured he could sleep peacefully, feeling the comfortable warmth of the autumn soil yet having fresh air to breath. Raindrops were falling all over the place but the lacerated shape of the uncountable piled up oak leaves formed a perfect umbrella. Little streams of water seemed to run down the valleys formed by the leaves, at times leading into smaller waterfalls when there was a greater distance between the different layers of the tree's foliage, eventually making a big jump once the water ran off the edge and was swallowed by the thirsty soil.

None of it concerned Tim, who, fully protected by nature, fell asleep, completely absorbed in his imagination.

IV

It was dark and the surroundings seemed different from the place they had met earlier. There wasn't a tree, a bench or a river. Or at least they couldn't see one as the weather was wet and the sun appeared to have retreated permanently. The labyrinthine alleys made orientation difficult. Time and again it was rumbling, sometimes thunder was near, and other times it was far. Mana wasn't really comfortable. It was a strange feeling. Somehow known and belonging to her, but still somehow foreign. She didn't know how to deal with it yet.

Mana wasn't alone; there was a familiar face that she recalled seeing before. Marc was also struggling with this place. He rarely came here, and every time his self-assuredness left him for a moment, because nothing seemed tangible, everything was in a different form than what he was used to. Nevertheless it seemed to be an important place. Maybe he would get used to it over time.

WINTER

Zen Garden

Mana's head seemed to buzz after a busy day at work. All the tasks and deadlines were weighing on Mana's body, leaving her almost no chance to take a deep breath as she was trying to finish as many of her assignments as possible.

There were some particular calming childhood memories that Mana liked to recall whenever she was overwhelmed by the busy world. Of all the days that Mana had spent with her grandparents when growing up, one particular memory that she liked to draw upon was observing her grandfather in his traditional Japanese garden.

Sleeping in as Mana was used to doing during her holidays; she would grab one of her favourite novels after finishing her breakfast and find a comfortable seat on the veranda. Following her grandfather's example, the first thing she would do as she stepped out into the still fresh autumn morning air was to take a deep breath, bow until she could reach her feet with her hands and then reach for the sky with the very same. Pulling her muscles gently and moving all her limbs, she felt re-energized, as if she were recharging her batteries. Being a man of few words, Mana's grandfather would briefly raise his head from what he was doing and greet her with 'good morning my dear'. The sun was still a little weak but as the fog slowly disappeared the intense autumn colours appeared. The contrast of golden colours with the blue of the sky was just amazing – a gift.

Preparing the plants for autumn, Mana's grandfather would spend his days trimming bushes and trees, cutting wilted flowers and collecting dry leaves from the ground. It was also the time of year when he would renew the small karensansui garden made of tiny rocks and gravel in one area surrounding the house. It was an exercise that looked like practising calligraphy, as her grandfather moved a wooden stick through the gravel surrounding the carefully made rock arrangements in a smooth movement with his entire body.

Completely absorbed by his work, he barely spoke to anyone during the day except for when he was asked something by either his wife or his granddaughter. It almost seemed that he was in a meditative state. Perfectly balanced and content with himself, he unconsciously practised calmness, refined his mindfulness and kept his focus on what he was doing. Nowadays, unfortunately, Mana rarely observed such devotion to work. For her grandfather it appeared to be completely natural. For Mana, the state of perfection and the level of aesthetics in her grandfather's garden was the expression of his attitude and mind-set. Nothing seemed to be subjected to force; all was in the place foreseen by the universe. What a privilege.

OPEN DRAWERS

Marc had had another restless night. His mind produced an action-like, fast paced set of frames of thought, which kept him awake nearly all night long. It seemed like he had a lot of unfinished stories that were occupying him.

His mum once told him that thoughts are kept in drawers. If closed properly they won't bug us, if not, chances are high that they will. Open drawers always pose the risk that one might injure a finger when attempting to quickly tidy up and close all of them. It seemed to be similar for his thoughts, Marc thought, recalling his mum's words. While Marc had overcome some of his worries and apparently successfully stored them in the drawer containing the settled thoughts, his subconscious was working hard on all the other stuff that he couldn't just brush aside. Despite all the vivid images which appeared during his restless sleep, he wasn't quite able to figure out what was bugging him the most. Was it the unresolved situation with Laura? The pressure at work or his own expectations that he could not live up to?

It required courage to pull the half-closed drawer fully open, face the unpleasant thoughts and work on them before being able to close the matter.

But restless as the night was, Marc didn't feel like he had any spare energy to do so at the moment. Nevertheless, another night like this wasn't a pleasant outlook either.

Maybe another round of jogging at the lake would get his thoughts going before heading to breakfast to be ready for work on time.

REACHING FOR THE STARS

It was 4.30 am on a cold winter morning, the night was still dark and dawn seemed ages away. Tim was very sleepy but his parents had told him that they would get up early to depart for their winter holiday in Austria.
Wearing multiple layers of clothes he felt comfortably warm and it was almost like still being in bed under his duvet. In fact he was already tightly secured in the rear seat of his parents' car while waiting for them to finish loading the luggage into the boot.
It didn't take long before they started their journey and Tim was half awake one moment and close to dozing off the next. Barely realizing what was happening around him, Tim was in his imaginative world of dreams, picturing where this journey would take him.
Ever since Tim had developed an interest in physics the universe had amazed him. He thought that aspiring to be an astronaut would satisfy his curiosity and would allow him to venture into that unknown space one day.
Still feeling the acceleration of the car, Tim's eyes were drawn to something lining the road in the tunnel which appeared to be an infinite number of glowing white

pearls closely arranged one after the other. Passing quicker and quicker, Tim wondered what it would be like to leave Mother Earth to venture into the dark. Would the force propelling him forward have the same rhythm as his pulsating heart that was filled with excitement?

Completely absorbed in his dream, Tim was already approaching the Milky Way. All the twinkling stars were lined up, and a variety of colours, shapes and sizes struck him that he was eager to touch. How would it feel to touch those heavenly bodies? Would they be cold, warm, hot, burning, smooth, sharp, soft or solid? What would it be like to float up there? As quiet as in his parents' car? Would there be any smells or flavours to tickle his nose?

As the dream continued, Tim imagined reaching out for the stars while travelling at lightning speed. Could he tickle the stars while moving his hands across them? Would he leave a trace in the sky as if moving his fingers through fine grains of sand? What would he want to draw for people on planet Earth to see?

COLD DECELERATION

Mana was out for an early lunch today. It had been snowing ever since she woke up this morning. She was headed for the harbour where the fishing boats were arriving, one of her favourite spots with benches right on the pier.

For lunch she had packed some hot seaweed soup with tofu and some grilled pieces of fish, which her mum had prepared early that morning. It was a quiet morning as the week was coming to an end and everybody's energy seemed to be nearing a low level just before the weekend arrived.

Tightly wrapped up with an alpaca hat covering her black long hair, Mana sat on a bench that was already powdered white with the snow. The steam rising from her hot soup fogged up her glasses temporarily and made the snowflakes melt right in front of her eyes.

While enjoying the homemade dishes she watched the people on the road. They seemed to move determinedly from one building to the next. Entering warm malls then exiting to the cold the next moment. Back to the office after lunch then out into the cold for the weekend.

As determined as they wished to be, Mana wondered whether they were aware of the urgency that they placed in their daily lives. It seemed that only with the snow people started to rethink their pace. It forced them to slow down.

The snow appeared to deaden all the noise of the hectic world. Flake by flake, the noise disappeared as if someone had stuck pieces of cotton wool into people's ears with each flake that fell. Conversations sounded softer, horns didn't honk as loud, traffic lights didn't seem to flash that strongly and buildings became rounder with snow covering the edges. How peaceful the world became when covered in all the white snow. It made Mana feel calmer, even though she was in fact desperately longing for some excitement in her life.

Time to go back and finish up her work before the weekend.

CONSCIENTIOUSNESS AT STAKE

Marc desperately needed some fresh air. It was Thursday afternoon and he was supposed to fly back home in three hours. Laura was already waiting for him to return. Sitting in his favourite spot, he was thinking how to explain to Laura that he might only return tomorrow, as there were some urgent issues to attend to that his client had just informed him of.

In fact Marc was very demoralized about the way things had progressed. Everything had started to annoy him. He had had enough of sitting at barely two office desks with six of his colleagues as the client hadn't provided more space for them to work. Everyone was trying to focus on their tasks while left and right people were either pretending to be busy with their smartphones or vigorously gesticulating during their phone calls. But what frustrated him even more were the conflicting expectations that he needed to deal with, also within his own team.

Already struggling to stay focused in his private life, Marc didn't know how to best manage the differing expectations. Dealing with his client's expectations was one thing but dealing with contradicting expectations from different stakeholders was something new to him. And on top of that, he was bothered by the situation in his own team. Marc was hoping for some thoughtful advice from his boss but all he had to say was "Don't take it so serious Marc!" Well, if he hadn't taken things seriously in the past would he be here today? In school he had learnt to deliver and live up to the highest expectations, and now in the corporate world he should just deliver less? It seemed like a tough lesson ahead of him, managing the expectations of others and himself seemed to be a fine line to walk.

He wasn't quite sure yet how to move forward, but looking for inspiration among his senior colleagues he was disappointed to pre-dominantly find resignation, a laissez-faire attitude and risk-minimizing but self-deceiving ignorance. It wasn't exactly what he strived to incorporate in his decision-making process and leadership style as he doubted that such a stance could ever form a solid economic foundation for the future.

A TIN OF TIME

After her Russian class Cassiopeia sat in the hallway of the linguistic faculty with her classmate Celia who had brought along some homemade cookies. Whenever Celia opened the tin a tempting smell of fresh butter cookies rose up to Cassiopeia's nose and she failed to resist the urge to grab another one, and another one, and a final one.

In her usual state of philosophical curiosity, Cassiopeia's mind was struck by a chameleonic thought. What if people could be given a tin of time? A tin which would give the presentee an extra hour of time during that day or an extra day in a week, a month or a year? What an easy way out it could be in times when people always run out of time. Tempted by the 'scent' of extra time people would open the tin of time and try to quickly close it again in order not to lose any of the extra time they had just been given. But once you opened the tin of time you would have to use it, you couldn't 'pause' and then 'play' again. Time wouldn't wait once the tin had been opened, like in real life.

How would one be able to give someone a tin of time in the first place? Would it be available for purchase? How much would a priceless tin of time cost? Cassiopeia disliked the idea of time as a tradable good. Affluent contemporaries would certainly take advantage of such an opportunity and she dare not imagine how buying up all the tins of time would affect the less wealthy population.

Maybe a tin of time could only be given to someone by trading some of one's own time? This sounded more viable to Cassiopeia than her first thought. A finite good like everyone's time seemed to become infinite once shared. To Cassiopeia, giving someone a tin of time would essentially mean sharing a dedicated part of time with someone else.

But this led Cassiopeia to yet another question: would she trade her own time for others? Maybe it would depend on what the presentee was going to do with the time they 'received'? Would they cram in as many activities into that given extra time as they would do for the rest of their life? Or would they be more deliberate in their choice since the extra time was scarce? It appeared to be contradictory as time was scarce anyway and you never knew when you might run out of it. Cassiopeia wasn't sure which approach was more likely with the lucky presentees.

SCENT CATCH

Tim was sad. Tomorrow his school was going on a fieldtrip to a well-known chocolate manufacturer. He had been looking forward to it for weeks but now Clara was sick and would most likely not be going on the excursion. He would have loved to watch the blending, mixing and refining of the ingredients, witnessing the conching and tempering of the chocolate mass before it was eventually filled into different moulds and shapes. What kind of different scents would fill the air? Together with Clara he wanted to discover the world behind the doors of the chocolate factory while holding her tightly.

He already wasn't very motivated at school today since his buddy was missing. But only one more class today and he could go home and prepare his bag for tomorrow. It was time for science. Maybe he could ask his science teacher whether there was a way of capturing smells so that he could not only take back some chocolate for Clara but also some of the amazingly rich and sweet smell of chocolate in the factory. At least that was what he pictured in his mind.

He was disappointed to learn that the teacher said there wasn't any simple way of taking a snapshot of a scent as it all happens in our nose and brain. Hmmm.

Not really paying attention to the teacher who was explaining how they would grow crystals in the lab, Tim's mind started wandering. There it was! He would just take some of those tiny glass bottles from the lab and seal them once he captured some of the smell in the chocolate factory!

Unfortunately, this plan didn't work well. Tim was caught red-handed as he was trying to sneak the tiny glass bottles into his school bag after class. Would he now also have to miss the excursion tomorrow?

TRAPPED

For once Marc wasn't restless or unable to sleep because of his worries or work but because of the moaning coming from the neighbouring hotel room. Though unwanted it diverted Marc's attention and tickled his imagination in the middle of the night. It was something that couldn't be controlled and yet, because it was kind of an obvious secret behind doors, it attracted Marc's attention.

It reminded him of Laura and how much he missed her. How he was longing for the tender strokes of her hands, the warmth of her body and intimacy with the one he loved but seemed to be losing.

How is it that sometimes thoughts seem to go in circles, with humans unable to refocus or stop paying attention to certain things, in this case sounds? Why do some of our senses and perceptions dominate and appear to be beyond our control?

As the noises of pleasure intensified, Marc's sensations did too. Like watching a well-shot love scene in his own mental cinema, which showed some, but not all of the details to continue teasing our curiosity, Marc was waiting for the culmination of things. With it the tension in his body rose, sleep was gone and his mind was fully engaged with what he imagined to be a scene of joy loaded with hormones and desire.

THE NIGHT IS MINE

Cassiopeia was turning restlessly in her bed. Her mind just didn't want to rest; it was producing a firework of thoughts which wouldn't be quiet. No matter what she tried, she was somehow completely alert though at the same time desperate to sleep. Random scenes of the movie she had watched with her friend Celia appeared in front of her inner eye, mixed with worries about the upcoming exams, arguments with her mum, headlines from the newspaper, and snapshots of memories from her recent holidays. A never-ending flow of neural firing.

Cassiopeia decided to give in to her restlessness and got up from her bed. She opened the window blinds and made herself comfortable on the window ledge, curling herself up in her fleecy blanket. The night was crystal clear and tickling cold, and she could almost hear nature freezing. With her breath clearly visible, inhaling and exhaling made Cassiopeia feel like a steam train. Looking at all the stars in the sky, resembling the lunatic greatness of the universe,

Cassiopeia's mind became speechless. Filled with astonishment, she slowly felt calmness settling in.

It was her night. The night that Cassiopeia would witness Ison. Like a strip of light painted by a skilful artist across the earth's black velvet ceiling, the tail of Ison was clearly visible. Now she recalled that astronomers around the world had been reporting about the upcoming event. What had been travelling for a million years now became visible and invisible within hours. What was built to last, a millennium old, slowly disappeared. Everything follows a cycle, no end, just now beginnings.

CONNECTED YET ALONE

Ruth and Walter didn't quite understand all the fuss their grown-up children Peter and Bettina were making about the recent developments in social media. All these services seemed so alien to them, particularly since the users were connected yet alone. Talking about their grandchildren, Ruth and Walter realized how much social structures had changed in the last few years. When they grew up, social structures were often collectivistic in nature – now, these structures had apparently been replaced by other types of network, but they weren't quite sure whether those new networks were able to cater for the social needs of human beings. Could they be a substitute on an equal footing with collectivistic family structures?

When Ruth and Walter grew up, they never questioned that family and social structures limited personal freedoms and the degree of choice by cultivating certain expectations. Now based on what their children told them, the new kind of social networks left people with lots of independence and room for choice about how closely linked and integrated one wanted to be.

But in reality these new structures were insufficient and wouldn't provide the same support as more traditionally collectivistic social structures in communities and families. Did people, including their own children, realize their dependence on a structure that was no longer fulfilling its purpose?

With our technological means we can maintain friendships around the globe, something that Walter himself appreciates since he worked internationally. But can this web of friends provide the same support in difficult times as the close-knit social network that Ruth and Walter grew up with? Growing up in a household with four and then three generations, Ruth and Walter both learned to value the primal trust of older generations and the light-heartedness of the youngest generation whenever they faced a challenging situation in life. Will the virtual web provide the same support when we want to bounce on it? They weren't quite sure and it worried them since they thought they had passed on some of these invaluable principles to their children.

BURDEN OF CHOICE

Recalling the discussions from the family gathering yesterday, Mana had one thing in mind – choice. There were so many options to choose from yet choice didn't make people happier. Particularly if they always wondered whether there was a better path than the one they had just chosen.

For Mana it was a constant dispute between knowing that every opportunity had a shelf life and the courage required to make a brave choice. The words of her relatives saying that she was too choosy were still bouncing around in her head as she returned to work.

WORLD'S QUICKEST FACTORY

Tim hadn't been in school for nearly two weeks. The seasonal flu had kept him in bed for many days. He still didn't really feel fit yet but he was much better than a few days ago and he didn't want to miss school any longer. He sat in the corner of the schoolyard with his friend Clara. Though she came to visit him once while he was sick they hadn't see each other for what felt like ages. Clara's mum had advised her daughter not to visit Tim too often while he was sick, otherwise she would end up having to stay in bed too.

Tim was glad to be in the fresh air, at least for the short break, as his nose was still pretty blocked and with the warm air in the classroom it was difficult to breath. Enjoying the fresh air as much as he could, Tim told Clara what he learnt from the doctor the other day. He was still fascinated about what he now thinks was the world's quickest factory. Tim learned that the flu and all the things that came with it are caused by an organism called a virus. The doctor told him to imagine a round bulky ball that enters our body through our nose or mouth. Since this ball is foreign to our body, at some point it will be picked up by something like a police patrol which keeps an eye on what enters our bodies.

If we are lucky, the police patrol will remember those balls from earlier encounters and will know what to do with them immediately. In that case, Tim excitedly explained to Clara who was chewing her snack, he wouldn't have been sick for so many days.

But in Tim's case the virus was new and the police didn't know what to do about the intruders yet. In order to make the viruses innocuous, the police would have to lock them up and eventually dispose of them. But these round bulky balls weren't that easy to lock up and unless there was a specific prison cell for them, they would still cause us to fall sick. Clara wasn't clear why Tim was saying our body was the world's quickest factory, but Tim reassured her that she would understand in a minute. As long as the prison cells for the viruses aren't available, the viruses will travel all around our bodies. The police will try to stop them everywhere, but unless there is a way to lock them up, it won't be easy to tie them down. With policemen running all over our body, we start to feel tired. Trying to get a clear picture of what the intruders look like, the police patrols rush from one place to another, causing us to have a headache. As soon as the police have a more or less clear picture about the size and shape of the uninvited guests, they order workers to start mining for the required materials to build the locks. Blasting away and collecting the required materials is what causes us to cough. Along with it comes a feeling of growing pains because workers drag the materials from all over our body.

Once all the required materials are in one place, other workers weld them together according to the description of the viruses provided by the police. The welding itself causes our body temperature to rise which is called a fever Tim said, if he remembered the doctor's words correctly. Usually, the whole process of building such cells takes a few days, and then another few days when the police hunt for the viruses and lock them all up.

The school bell rang; it was time to get back to the classroom. Clara was still holding her snack, with her mouth wide open, looking at Tim with a gaze that indicated disbelief.

EXCUSES NOT REASONS

Cassiopeia thought she was adult enough to handle everything that life threw at her, but the recent argument between her parents that she had witnessed proved her wrong. Maybe because it was the first time she had heard them screaming at each other endlessly in such a relentless way.

And how silly it was what they had argued about. But neither of them wanted to give in, so instead they continued with their accusations. To Cassiopeia it sounded like lots of frustration had accumulated and now it was being released all in one go.

Recalling what she had witnessed appeared totally foreign to Cassiopeia as she had always thought of her parents as a loving couple who never argue. But what she had heard shattered this image. Her parents were threatening to leave each other after 20 years of happy marriage.

And the argument only started because of an unfinished pond in the garden. It has been a never-ending project of her dad's, which was like an inkblot on a beautiful white piece of paper. It was highly visible but not the way Cassiopeia's mum wanted it to be because everything else in their garden was well arranged. It was hard for Cassiopeia to believe that this unfinished piece of gardening work could be the potential trigger of her parents' divorce.

What started with a difference in opinion about the finishing of the pond ended in a flood of tears, where statements like 'you don't care about me', 'you are always stubborn' or 'you never help to do this' were thrown around.

What astonished Cassiopeia were not the statements themself but the realization that those might just be excuses and not the real reason for the fight. Why would kids be cruelly direct about what they felt and thought while adults couldn't? What seemed to come out of a good intention to prevent each other from being hurt suddenly appeared to be a defect of adulthood.

It was barely noon but Marc was already desperate for a nap. Coffee hadn't helped or fresh air. And concentration was inexistent this week. Marc was glad it was already Thursday and he was just hours away from flying back home. Hopefully the familiar environment and his own bed would allow him to have some restorative nights ahead.

In the past few days, many thoughts had been weighing heavily on him. The still unresolved situation with Laura and all the issues at work made Marc feel like his mind was being fed by a funnel of worries and fears beyond his control. And all this kept him awake at night even though he often found himself dead tired and completely exhausted by the time he went to bed. Even if he fell asleep quickly, it was just a matter of time until he was completely absorbed in dreams where his subconscious was trying to make sense of everything that had happened. Rather than enjoying the vivid and extremely rich pictures that Marc dreamt of, he wished he had a button to switch off his mind temporarily. Maybe that would also have helped him to regain his gut feeling. Ever since he had felt his mind being overloaded, he no longer had a chance to rely on his gut feelings. Maybe it was also his unbalanced diet and his lack of appetite that contributed to this momentary incapability to rely on what he felt. But as he wasn't sure whether to blame it on the bacteria in his gut or on something else, all he wished for now was a long deep sleep to recharge.

No Horizon

It was Sunday morning and Tim had just woken up. From his bed he looked straight ahead outside the windows. His three window partitions with the fine middle sections looked like a grid. Traceries lined the edges of the frosted windows. It must have been a really cold night, but the sun was slowly rising and the view was stunning – a stale blue sky, golden yellow sunrays and white snow-covered surroundings. Though he was still in his warm bed, Tim could exactly imagine the crisp fresh air loaded with the taste of snow.

Still somnolent, Tim heard his parents far away as they were preparing breakfast. He could hear them handling the cutlery, plates and coffee machine. The smell of fresh pastries and bread hadn't reached his nostrils yet, otherwise he would have been out of bed quickly – but instead he stayed and continued daydreaming.

Sitting half upright in his bed, leaning against the headboard, Tim felt as if he were the captain on a huge containership. In an instant his bedroom turned into a bridge from where, by his mere thoughts, he was steering this giant of the ocean. Water formed a symmetrical V shape starting from the bow and then continued left and right of the vessel as it moved forward.

Scanning the horizon for potential obstacles, Tim recalled his science class from the other day. They had learnt that Mother Earth was a spherical shape and that many years ago there were people who claimed that the Earth was a flat disk. Now he knew it was the shape of a globe. So, if the shape of the Earth was like a round ball, and Tim was looking out of his window, why could he only see to the horizon and no further? Why couldn't he see outer space at the other end? Maybe some special binoculars would allow him to see beyond the horizon? Tim was curious to find out. What else could we discover if our sight wasn't limited?

EYES FAR AHEAD

What an encouraging encounter. It was Thursday again and for once Marc had not left his client's office disappointed. He had met a new member of the executive management who was usually based in the Middle East, though he originally called India his home. Marc felt he was an extraordinary man.

In the critical discussions, for which all the regional area heads had travelled to the headquarters and where progress and the next steps of Marc's project were discussed, Marc often found himself sunken in thoughts. Not because he was day-dreaming, mentally absent or ignorant to what was being presented and argued, but because he was reflecting deeply about what was at stake. He sat very upright and made notes carefully as if he were arranging his thoughts before putting them on paper. His handwriting was firm and very distinct. His eyes were very clear, sparkling and looking far ahead.

When he spoke, his colleagues immediately went quiet, paid attention to what he had to say and listened respectfully. Even when he didn't speak, his presence was felt strongly. It was not an arrogant and surprised feeling but a promising and empowering one. Whenever discussions went off track, became unconstructive or emotional, his pacifying comments had a calming influence on the entire team. Contrary to his colleagues who were desperately clinging on to the existing way the firm operated, most likely being driven by personal fears of losing what they had, not what they were, this remarkable Indian man was embracing the upcoming changes as an opportunity, a unique chance for someone who wants to contribute, to make a difference and to shape what lies ahead. With his eyes pointing forward, his mind firm about what he had reflected on, this new colleague was exactly the type of visionary leader that the organization needed.

Marc was extremely pleased he had had the chance to meet Mr. Indra as they all called him. Hopefully he would be the catalyst to move things in the right direction. Standing in front of the mirror in the airport lavatory, Marc realized for the first time in months that he was carrying a smile on his face and not the usual cloudy mood and signs of exhaustion. What a week.

THE WORLD TURNING

Cassiopeia spent a few days of her study break in New York with her friend Celia. They were lucky to have got a seat on an inexpensive flight and were now surfing a couch in trendy Soho.

Unfortunately, their host's apartment didn't provide them with a clothes washing facility. While Celia promised to queue up for tickets to a special photography exhibition jointly organized by the New York Photography Institute and the Kodak Centre of Art, Cassiopeia was sitting in front of a washing machine in a laundromat on Fifth Avenue. While waiting patiently for her laundry to finish, Cassiopeia was observing the busy streets of New York. Facing the window and watching outside, ironically, Cassiopeia did not feel like she was sitting in a shop window herself but rather the opposite. It seemed to her that everything that was happening in front of her was happening in perfectly set up shop windows, confirming all her stereotypical assumptions that she had made prior to coming to NYC.

The cosmopolitan NYC habitants appeared to be perfectly dressed in the latest designer clothes as if they were display dummies that had just escaped from the hippest designer store around the corner.

The NYC police patrol at every other crossing was like a snapshot from the mock-up movie set in Hollywood. Sitting in their Chevys, she found them busy munching a burger, drinking coke from a huge paper cup while listening to the radio waiting for crimes to happen. With the citizens' loss of confidence in their own common sense, the angels in their blue uniforms had a lot to protect.

With her eyes observing the world and her ears busy with the monotonous sound of the laundry machine which kept turning and turning, Cassiopeia didn't hear the fire brigade rushing across Broadway until her view of NYC was blocked for an instant as the bright red yet old fashioned looking fire engine passed in front of the shop window.

As the monotonous sound resumed, Cassiopeia caught sight of yet another picturesque scene. A bunch of kids were impatiently gathering in front of a mobile ice cream/waffle store where temptations in all colours were sold. What a sweet life in such hustle and bustle. But who in NYC had kids anyway? Fashionably dressed New Yorkers rear dogs of all breeds that they pamper like their own kids. They spend many dollars in dog grooming stores like the one on the corner just opposite to where Cassiopeia was sitting and even join special parties that offer dance floors to both master and pet alike!

With the laundry machine having finished spinning and her change dropping noisily into a small metal tray, Cassiopeia was pulled out of her daydreaming state by one particular thought that remained in her mind - will the world ever stop turning if we all go on as we are doing?

A NOBLE VOCATION

Tim really liked the experimental days at school where his science teacher would make him and his classmates watch experiments attentively, eyes wide open, sometimes not realizing that their jaws had dropped and their mouths were open due to their astonishment.

This created an urge in Tim about his future occupation. He'd always found that his dad had a boring job; going to the office from early morning until late in the evening wasn't what Tim was looking for. He was sure he wanted to do something different, something more extraordinary. At first he thought he wanted to be an astronaut. Watching the world from outer space made everything seem so small and would put things into a different perspective. But somehow, despite the appealing view on planet blue, Tim found there could be even more excitement if he ventured into another profession.

What he really wanted was to be an inventor. Maybe not a crazy genius like some of the world's most outstanding contemporaries that he had heard of so far, but one that still makes a difference to 'normal' citizens' lives. Like his best friend Clara for example. With everyone trying to create something that will last forever, Tim wanted to create something that had a profound effect even though it only lasted for a few seconds, minutes or hours at the most.

What Tim wanted to invent was dreams. Dreams to inspire people. He thought the job of an inventor was a very challenging but also rewarding occupation. Nevertheless, he was confident that if he did his work as a dream writer diligently, he would make a difference to the world. If his inventions encouraged people to pursue their dreams with a firm belief and turn them into reality that would certainly be a noble vocation.

NO EXCEPTION

Cassiopeia had just spent a rare evening watching TV. She had witnessed a very disturbing trend, which has been in her mind for quite some time.

Cassiopeia was of the firm conviction that human beings are just one part of nature's clockwork. Daring to treat them as an exception was the first step towards taking apart a well-working equilibrium, which follows its own laws, many of which are still beyond our reach or understanding despite centuries of scientific research. Knowing that flower petals are usually arranged in a perfect order and number, which can even be described by a mathematical formula wasn't enough. Yet many believe in the supremacy of Homo sapiens.

What Cassiopeia saw on TV was a heart-breaking documentary about retired circus elephants, which were brutally removed from their habitat for the entertainment of people in circuses. Picking a random elephant from its highly social family context left the remaining family members mourning their lost contemporary. The removal from their families was just the first step of a long ordeal ahead of them, as the elephants would first be transferred from the wild to the backstage of a circus. With cruel methods of tying and beating, circus members would try to teach the elephants how to entertain an audience. Not surprisingly, with metal hooks hitting their temples, the elephants learnt over time and remembered. This torture lasted for decades or at least as long as the circus existed, leaving the protagonists in a fragile state with behavioural abnormalities.

At one point, fortunate elephants were adopted by zoo keepers who dedicated their time to rehabilitating what others had caused. As is commonly known, elephants have an excellent memory and despite their painful journey they didn't lose their minds. Back in a park for rehabilitation, many of them would meet fellow elephants with similar fate from the same herd or even the same family. Recognising their relatives after years of painful circus work, they might have a glimpse of hope and enjoy a peaceful retirement from an occupation that they never deliberately chose but that was forced upon them by someone who thought they knew better about their place in the world.

LIGHTS FOR THE ANTHILL

Tim wanted to stay in bed. It was still completely dark outside, so why should he go to school at this hour? But his mum didn't leave him any opportunity to continue sleeping as it was already 6:30 and therefore he had to get up and get ready for school. The only thing that motivated him at this point in time was the smell of freshly baked bread, croissants or alike which somehow found the way to his room and his sensitive nostrils. He loved eating breakfast and enjoyed the slightly warm and crunchy baked goods, the cold but nutty butter and of course, all the different types of home-made jam. His mum always had to remind him not to eat too much of the jam and that the main part of his breakfast was his bowl of cereal and the bread, not just the jam.

The night was still pitch black when Tim reluctantly stepped outside the house. Some of the houses in the area were still dark, while others were lit up and the light appeared to be bright and warm, a strong contrast to the cold and obscure night. As Tim was walking to the centre of the town where the school was, he realized that wherever there was light, there was hustle and bustle. He felt like he was in an anthill. There were different warrens and there were occasional places where there was more light, other anthills or complete darkness.

All these adult ants seemed to head off to work with a purpose in mind or a task assigned, just following the light as if someone had switched on a button and everything started moving all at once. Some appeared to be genuinely busy and others were pretending to be busy but in fact enjoyed some time dreaming.

As he walked along he came across other anthills, where all those ants were already busily moving around, surrounded by other ants and light of course, but somehow it was covered in a cap of darkness. What would all those ants do without light? They would have to wait until dawn to start moving around. He wondered who came up with the idea of work anyway; he couldn't quite understand yet why humans would feel bored if they didn't have to go to work. Would he, one day, be one of those ants as well? So far, he didn't really want to be. He was happy to go to school every day and learn something new, except for when it was as dark as today.

SAILS SET FOR A STORM

There it was. Unexpected but still expected after the past few months. Laura had insisted on a break and Marc was devastated. The moment he put down the phone to Laura his emotions and thoughts rushed through the entirety of his body like an electric shock. His blood was running through his veins at lightning speed and his head was spinning. It felt like wind was blowing at him from all directions and the noise was increasing as if someone was playing relentlessly with the amplifier.

Yet another challenge in life – Marc thought – discouraged and powerless. He felt like his mind and body were trying to maintain a certain direction, while the wind was suddenly blowing full force in a different one. When life is about to challenge our focus, sails are set for a storm with or without our contribution.

It made Marc feel helpless but he knew, somehow, he would have to find a way forward. He recalled the encounter he had had with the monk in the park. He reminded him that, at the end of the day, many things combined such as our will, our skills, the water's current and the direction of the wind determine where we are heading, but we are still the ones navigating the boat even under those seemingly adverse conditions. Our thoughts are our ultimate power but also our limitations at the same time. What should he do next with all this pain settling in?

SHARING IS BELIEVING

Cassiopeia left her lectures early today as she was just too frustrated with her professors who didn't have a constructive teaching style. It was one-way communication without any interaction between the pupil and teacher. No attention was given to an enriching dialogue; there was no consideration of the student's understanding or skills, but rather a blanket approach to disseminating information in the same way it has always been shared, regardless of the audience receiving it. Just pouring the knowledge onto the students regardless of their readiness to absorb it and not paying attention to the individual differences of the pupils.

As she headed home, Cassiopeia's annoyance subsided and she recalled the teaching style in Tibet, which she had witnessed while teaching English during her first volunteer stay. She particularly recalled the complex relationships between masters and their pupils with regards to the beliefs that were shared. Those masters seemed to have extraordinary capabilities to make their hidden knowledge tangible for others by the mere choice of appropriate words, thereby judging which of their students were ready to receive which piece of know-how. If they found that the pupil wasn't ready, they'd wait. This was something that seemed much more sustainable than the "works for all" kind of approach. One could say such an approach was a luxury but at the end of the day our education system, in which our teachers make the crucial difference, was the most important for the foundation of the prosperous development of a country's economy.

I

What a vibrant environment. A pulsating yet calming rhythm. This was where Enrique felt comfortable, though sometimes his impulsiveness also got him into trouble occasionally. But usually, if he followed his core, he was rewarded with authentic encounters. Especially now, as the first bits of green started to appear and the rejuvenated surroundings became visible.

Ruth and Walter had been at home here for quite some time. But it took them many years to reach. The roads were winding and often discouraging but eventually their firm beliefs and persistence prevailed. There wasn't any other place like it. Whatever originated here had the power to move mountains out of the way, cross oceans within seconds and reach for the stars without the fear of falling. It was somehow filled with an inherent courage, which nature also displayed after its white sleep.

SPRING

WANDERING

Here I am again, Mana thought after a long day at work. While everybody seemed to be heading somewhere, Mana headed nowhere except for her mind. Mana sat on a bench in the park near her office. Surrounded by green instead of office cubicles and concrete walls is usually the first time in the day when she feels at peace. At least until her mind starts to wander. While a stream of people flooded the surrounding roads like water flooded valleys, Mana was astonished by the modern slaves of capitalism seemingly heading home after an exhausting day of chasing for the ever-present shareholder value.

Her round dark brown eyes, the rouge on her cheeks and the fashionable mushroom haircut said nothing about Mana's struggle. A struggle that had left her lonely and absorbed in her thoughts for many months. That's when she usually came to find a moment of quietness in the middle of this park. Spring was just around the corner and Mana found comfort observing nature waking up after the arctic sleep during winter. Though Mana occasionally sat here during the white period of the year, she preferred the warmer months when shoots forced their way up to catch the first rays of the then still weak sun.

Now, when the day was ending, Mana was off to catch this serenity in the middle of the concrete jungle before the sun set and left her with the choice to either become accustomed to the darkness or to be hooked by the lights of the industrial world where the stars were not visible most of the time because light pollution took its toll.

For many early nights just after work Mana sat on the bench alone. Before she came here she went to her favourite shrine nearby. Absorbed by her daily work and trying to keep up with the pace in the office, she hadn't managed to leave on time. Reaching the shrine, the only choice left was to pray from the outside in front of the big wooden doors, which were guardians of the peacefulness and spirituality. Neatly dressed for work, Mana had prayed for the same thing for many months. Folding her hands and closing her eyes she addressed her personal wishes to the deity.

Approaching thirty, her family members kept asking her to find a husband. Whenever there was a family gathering she would be asked to bring her still inexistent boyfriend along. Whenever asked, she felt she was being blamed for not being successful in this domain of her life. But it wasn't her deliberate choice. Many of Mana's friends were either in relationships or already married. Only a few shared the same fate. Yet she hoped to be noticed by the special someone one day soon.

Brick after Brick

Her newly discovered interest in neuroscience made Cassiopeia want to rummage through scientific journals which were available in the library. Cassiopeia had recently read an interesting article about the process of learning. Now that she was sitting across the road, waiting for her friend to finish school, she was making her own thoughts about how humans learn.

Visiting a close school friend for the weekend that had moved to Wimbledon, Cassiopeia was enjoying the beginning of spring in one of the community parks. In the light of the sun, the green of the park was a well-balanced contrast to the red-coloured British town houses surrounding the area. As for many other architectural human creations, the British town houses were constructed by neatly stacking brick after brick on top of each other.

This seemed like a perfect metaphor for what Cassiopeia thought of the human learning process. Basically, right from the moment when we arrive in the seemingly cold world after leaving our mother's womb, learning starts, in whatever way. By making a mistake, touching something, hurting ourselves, being taught or socialized consciously and unconsciously we collect brick after brick and start building our own collection of experiences.

Starting off with bare land, Cassiopeia was sure we must have learned the basics of architecture while still in the womb. How, otherwise, would we be able to arrange brick after brick once we are born?

Unaware of our predispositions, we lay the foundations on land that wasn't deliberately chosen by us but as a matter of destiny will form the basis of our architectural work from now on. While some 'architects' will complete their foundations in due time, others might take longer. As with all new buildings, constructing a tower of learning from scratch always appears to rise quickly.

Cassiopeia was sure that although there might be something like good architectural standards or designs, the stacking of bricks was a truly subjective process resulting in a unique structure as individual as our fingerprints.

With the responsibility for laying the bricks being entirely our own, Cassiopeia recognized that during the tenure of our life we will have different brick suppliers who all supply bricks in various shapes and of different quality. Some bricks will actively be brought to us, while others will have to be sought. While in the early stages our suppliers might be parents, other children and teachers, they are complemented with friends, partners, colleagues and bosses at a later stage. At other times, certain memorable moments or incidents could also provide us with exotically shaped bricks, be it eating sand for the first time while playing in the sandbox and realizing that it won't do us any good, learning a new language or acquiring the knowledge of how to prepare nearly lost household remedies from our grandparents.

Some 'architects' might know exactly what their work ought to look like, while others make their design according to the bricks they have to hand. Certainly, the surrounding circumstances will play a crucial role. Expectations might have an influence on how the design should look and the composition of the soil might determine how quickly and how high we can stack our bricks.

At one point, the arrangements of bricks might be square in shape, relatively flat, cylindrical or rather tall. Disregarding the shape the structure was about to reveal, for Cassiopeia the repetitive arrangement of bricks would also entail learning. Merely stacking the bricks will not lead us anywhere as the tower could become unstable or collapse partially. Building complex architecture might need much more time and will require continuous efforts to perfect our existing skills while acquiring new ones.

Becoming more adept in stacking the bricks, some of the 'architects' might become complacent. Others might suddenly be unsure about whether they want to continue what they initially considered to be their architectural masterpiece or whether they'd rather start building something new from scratch. While a third group of architects, eager to fulfil their destiny, will have to be patient in order not to risk the sustainability of their brick laying.

In any case, stacking brick after brick in a personally meaningful way, Cassiopeia realized that two traits distinguish 'architects' from 'architects'. Never, was her first thought, should an 'architect' be complacent about his work to the extent that the context of the building is isolated from its surroundings. There is always a way to improve what has been built, to make it steadier or to add another collection of bricks, allowing a clearer view of the horizon.

Secondly, though not always easy, we should always be grateful for the building materials we receive. No matter how oddly shaped the brick might be, or how unsuitable we find it for our architectural plans, Cassiopeia was sure, we can possibly never know in advance, that one day exactly that specific brick will make the difference.

As with all matters of neuroscience that Cassiopeia had encountered so far, she found the thoughts to be so enormously complex that she could spend endless hours reflecting on them. But by now an excited Lucie was standing in front of her, waiting for her so they could enjoy their time together.

Awakening Attraction

Whenever Mana went for lunch with her colleagues she realized how much they liked to talk. While apparently competing in a noodle slurping contest, which was all about pace, not a single one of them ever kept quiet. They seemed to forget that we were given two ears and only one mouth, maybe to emphasize the importance of the function of the former.

Only a few weeks ago Mana had decided to get fit again with a weekly run on Saturday mornings. Desperate to find a boyfriend, she was determined to take destiny in her own hands by making sure her slim and sporty body attracted the attention of her male contemporaries. It was during those runs that she had time to reflect on and digest her observations.

Pausing to do her stretching, placing her left heel on the bench and leaning her upper body forward to pull her toes she realized that the birds in the park were announcing the dawn of a new day. Delicate sounds of tiny filigree creatures filled our surroundings day by day. But who, she wondered, still cared these days to listen to those birds waking up in a world where only being heard seemed to count?

Maybe only the beggar awakening without an alarm clock on the bench next to her, who was grateful to have survived another night.

WE ARE IN CONTROL, AREN'T WE?

Busy reviewing the utilization reports of his consultants for the past month, Marc recalled an eye-opening discussion he had had with Sarah over a cup of coffee in the office today. Sarah had just got back from extended maternity leave. She proudly told Marc about her son's progress at the all-day nursery centre that she had sent him to. Apparently, and this was still hard for Marc to believe though he trusted Sarah, she had just received a report outlining her son's development. Wow – a report with detailed explanations and colourful charts including benchmarks? It seemed that everything was measured, compared and reported…general social skills, conflict resolution skills, motor skills, etc. Amazing. For each measured skill there was a graph outlining the average development of the peer group and then the performance of the individual.

Marc was shocked. He knew how much his bosses relied on reports but what he had learnt from Sarah was beyond his imagination. Kids just barely a few months old are evaluated and reports on their progress make us believe they have a certain character trait and are ahead or behind in their development of skills compared to others. For everything we need data, testimonials, reports, grading sheets and so forth. What has happened to our observations skills? Our ability to judge independently and confidently about what we see? Do we really believe that all these quantified metrics can help us to avoid the risks attributed to uncertainty in any kind of development?

OF SMALL AND BIG

It was yesterday that Tim was amazed by the size of things in this world. Now, on a break at school, after having just resumed school a month ago, he escaped his bullying friends by finding an empty bench in one of the corners of the schoolyard. Finishing his favourite snack packed by his mum every morning before he went off to school, his mind slipped away to yesterday afternoon. It had always been a highlight in his young life when he could enter the gigantic circus tent near his house. Of course, his mum wouldn't let him go alone, but even though he would walk alongside her, holding her hand tightly, his senses were busy with what was happening around him.

It started off with the smell of the sawdust as he walked around the tent from the entrance of the circus area, which would still be in his nose even days after his circus visit. The smell of the animals eagerly waiting in their cages for their turn. Goats, horses or elephants – Tim's nose was occupied with all the odorous molecules. What he liked about the circus was the colourfulness. Huge red and white stripes forming the tent of the circus from the outside, while inside, an infinite dark blue sky created a mystical yet joyful atmosphere. And then the lights sometimes warm yellow like a candle, and other times striking pink or flashing white lightning. His left hand in the tight grip of his mum's hand, Tim's right hand was holding on to the programme. It was time to take a seat. From the outside the tent appeared to be at least two houses high. Sitting on his wooden chair, Tim could barely make out the top of the roof where the acrobats were flying through the air. Here it was, the start of the circus being announced by the drums of the small orchestra somewhere in the corner.

Tim's jaw dropped and barely closed once until the bell rang for the break. Too impressed by the horse riders, too surprised by the fabulous magician and laughing out loud due to the jokes of the clowns, Tim hadn't realized how quickly the time had passed. Only when his nostrils started to smell nutty popcorn and sugar coated almonds did it dawn on him that it was time for some fresh air outside the tent. How unfortunate that the bell sounded like the school bell and somehow didn't fit with the one he remembered from last year's circus.

SPRING SHOOTS

For once Mana was not sitting on her favourite bench but instead lying down in the grass next to it. Comfortable on the fresh shoots of the grass which were still a little wet from the chilly night before, Mana was looking at the uncountable number of tiny dew drops which were shining as the first, still weak, sunrays appeared this morning. Reflecting the stale blue of the sky and the striking green of the grass, the seemingly infinite pearls of water of all sizes looked like small tiny globes. Globes like you would find in the geography lab at school, on key-chains or in pictures from outer space. With the noisy city yet to wake up, Mana turned her head to the side, her ear pressed against the soft ground trying to listen to the grass grow. Could she really hear it grow? How would it sound when the shoots forced their way up from the soil, extending themselves to grow bigger and bigger towards the sun?

Listening to the delicate yet cheerful voices of the birds excitedly twittering about the arrival of spring, Mana daydreamed about a surprising encounter yesterday on her way to work as she passed by the newly opened Sandwicheria. In her mind was the handsome man who appeared to be the shop owner but who she did not dare to ask out. It was the third time his gaze had left an unforgettable image with her which appeared in her mind as soon as it was idle. After the second time she swore to herself that whenever she saw him again she would gather all the courage she had and ask him out, even though she still didn't know how to approach him. No matter what phrase she thought of to start the conversation, none of them would work for approaching a stranger.

But the outlook of finally starting spring with a boyfriend made her so excited that she was enjoying lying in the grass even though it was still wet. Completely forgetting herself and her surroundings, she imagined what she would do if they finally had a chance to meet. With the temptingly sweet image in her mind, Mana suddenly noticed a previously unknown feeling that she thought she would never experience.

The heart pounding while her eyes were closed, Mana imagined lying besides her yet to be boyfriend, holding his hand while staring at the clear sky with him. Eager to know what the future would bring, they both looked for clues among the randomly twinkling heavenly objects.

THE WORLD IS MY CASTLE

Ruth and Walter had been invited to their new neighbours a few rows away in their quarter. They didn't know these newcomers yet, all they knew was that the property had been under construction for nearly two years. They hadn't followed the construction closely as it was out of their usual way. But when they received the invitation to the open house summer party they decided to give their new neighbours a chance to introduce themselves.

What they saw when they arrived at the venue after a short walk between the other houses was stunning. At first glance they were speechless. After that they were saddened and upset by the decadence that they witnessed as they were guided through the mansion. It was a luxurious three-story villa, which was totally misplaced in this part of what they considered a middle-class town. The architecture and interior design seemed to have followed one single principle – exclusivity, no matter at what cost. The entire house was filled with fine designer pieces. The dog kennel had a marble floor and heating. Pomp seemed to have no end. Even the buffet was filled with a lavish amount of finger food, which appeared to be right out of the marketing brochure of a highly exquisite catering supplier.

Ruth and Walter discovered hesitation in the eyes of all their fellow neighbours as they all tried to socialize. Growing up with endless opportunities, we seem to forget how privileged we are. It seems that if you only have a little you learn that a little bit is much more. Unfortunately, many are still tempted to build their castles without consideration for others, often forgetting that our lack of consideration leads to waste and leaves many in the world with hungry stomachs. And despite castles epitomizing material prosperity, happiness and satisfaction are scarce.

Homogeneity

Cassiopeia was in a state of wonder. Would there be a day when all human beings looked the same? A day when post-capitalist colonialism leads to unrestricted mobility around the globe, where languages are lost as generations fail to pass on the core of their cultural identity, where traditions become mere obligations rather than valuable heritage? Would there be a day when fine Asian facial features would complement fair Caucasian skin with muscular bodies from Africa? Would we have all longer second toes or a longer big toe? Would our eyes be as round and colourful as marbles or be shaped like a narrow filigree window to the world? Would we still argue about cultural differences when dealing with alien business counterparts? Would we all be paying with the same money or would we have started barter trading again?

Cassiopeia couldn't get to like the idea of a homogenous human population. It seemed like too much would be at stake. Why, she wondered, would we then be curious to discover what makes us different from others after all? On the other hand, not having to compare might be both pleasurable and painful. Striving to be the same or something different can be taxing, as you are not able to orientate yourself equally.

THE GIFT

Tim was excited. He was spending more and more time with his friend Clara. Though Clara bullied him sometimes when he dreamt in class, they got along very well. Usually they would spend the break munching their snacks packed by their caring mothers while sitting together on one of the benches in the schoolyard. Leaving the classroom, Tim realized that Clara was somehow nervous. He didn't know what was wrong with her until they sat down on the bench and Clara started looking for something in her snack bag. She pulled out a colourful envelope and proudly handed it over to Tim. At first Tim didn't know what to do with it until Clara, who by now was a little impatient, told him that he was invited for her 8th birthday party the coming Saturday at her parents' house.

Tim was happy to be invited and as Clara started telling him a little bit about the preparations that her mum had made, he was sure it would be lots of fun. Then suddenly Tim remembered that people usually receive a present for their birthday, and that he had just spent his savings on a new LEGO® kit the other day. What should he give Clara as a gift? His mum surely wouldn't let him go empty-handed, but he also didn't have much of his pocket money left. And since Clara always spent time with him, he wanted to give her something special. He decided to think it over during the next class. With class about to resume, Clara and Tim started walking back to the main building.

Recalling his noble aspiration to become a dream writer, it suddenly dawned on him that he could give it a go by giving Clara the gift of a dream. He still wasn't quite sure whether that was possible. Could he really give her a dream as a present? Happy about his glorious idea, Tim wondered what kind of dream he wanted Clara to have. And how could he wrap it? What kind of ribbon would he use? He knew Clara's favourite colour was violet. He would have to ask his mum. As excited as Tim was about it, he was also unsure when he realized he couldn't wrap a dream for Clara as it is something that happens in our mind. In the meantime he figured out what he wanted Clara to dream. They should appear as high-wire artists in his favourite circus! But how on earth could he get Clara to dream about that?

Tim found that sometimes it was very hard to remember the dreams he had during his sleep until the next morning, so how could he possibly give someone a particular dream as a gift? But then Tim also realized that some sections of his dreams were always clear and he could re-call them at any time of the day, like for example the smell of the sawdust in the circus tent. Maybe he should just wrap a little packet of sawdust for Clara? Would she dream of the circus then like he did?

He was still in doubt when his teacher reminded him that the class had started and he should pay attention.

Sparks

One more time. Mana was out for lunch and walked into her new favourite Sandwicheria with the handsome Italian shop owner behind the counter. She was utterly nervous as the shop didn't have a menu located on each table where one could choose without being subjected to other people's looks. Rather, in this shop, the daily offerings were beautifully written on a slate board behind the counter from which Mana was supposed to choose a panini. Mana was used to this concept from other stores, but as she stood at the counter with Paolo looking at her attentively while waiting for her to make her choice, she could feel a kind of tension rising within her. Not in a negative way, but rather a sensation of suppressed excitement. She finally made her choice randomly as she already felt like she had been standing there for ages. Paolo acknowledged her order with a smile on his face and his hands quickly started to assemble her sandwich. Mana couldn't take her eyes off his hands, which were moving around confidently. She was almost in a state of daydreaming when Paolo asked her whether there was anything else she would like.

Caught a little bit off guard, she was barely able to respond and only managed to say a brief 'no'. As Paolo was taking her cash and Mana was about to turn around Paolo gave her a small blank piece of paper and asked her if she could write down her name, phone number and email address as he was about to start a loyalty programme for his frequent customers, of which she was one. Mana was too astonished to think about whether this was Paolo's true intention or just a way to get her contact details. She blushed immediately but happily wrote down what he had asked for. Excited that he finally had her details, she took her sandwich and found a seat where she could still peak at the counter while eating. Realizing that Paolo might have asked for her details for a different reason than the mentioned loyalty programme, Mana wanted to see whether any of the other customers wrote something down on a piece of paper.

No one else did, but maybe today she was the only frequent customer? Excited and curious at the same time Mana left the shop once she had finished her lunch. She wasn't sure whether she would be able to focus on her work that afternoon. Her mobile phone would be lying next to her on her desk, constantly awaiting a message or a call from an unknown number that showed up on the screen.

IN OR OUT

Looking at the announcement of promotions Marc was surprised to see certain names on the list. Surprised on the one hand and not surprised on the other because some of the promoted colleagues were masters at positioning themselves on a battlefield where Marc only saw losers, particularly the cause and the corporation, most likely not the individuals, though, at least not all of them. Marc wasn't up for this game of power, politics and personal interests; he wanted to make a noticeable contribution to change. But his environment wanted him to believe that this was only possible if he joined in with the game, not if he opted out. Was that really so?

MESMERIZING BEAUTY

Enrique was on his way to the regional sales conference in Asia. Flying business class on long-haul flights meant he always boarded the aircraft early to make himself comfortable.

He was stunned when his neighbour appeared. At first he thought he was dreaming but even after pinching himself a few times the lady was still there. He must have been staring at her but he just couldn't stop looking at her. Her fine features appeared to be like those of a hand-made doll, which has been awarded the star prize for its beauty. Stunning round brown eyes of an unseen depth left room for thoughts about all the secrets one could discover. A well proportioned, perfectly symmetrical face, which would generally be considered boring, but in this case was part of the fascination. A small body with firm muscles, not at all appearing weak. What a mesmerizing beauty. Enrique was blown away. He didn't even realize that the stewardess was talking to him and had enquired about his meal preferences until she repeatedly said "sir…".

The unknown fellow traveller was unimpressed by Enrique's stares and her shyness, at least that was what Enrique guessed from her facial expression, did not leave any chance of her approaching him, therefore Enrique was ready to take his chance. But Enrique was disappointed as the unknown beauty only spoke Japanese and that was not part of his flattery vocabulary.

Enrique was too agitated to sleep. His neighbour didn't even wait for the evening service but got ready to rest straight away. Covered with the navy blue blanket provided by the airline, she was covered from head to toe. Only part of her neck was visible as it rested on the pillow. It looked so tender and Enrique felt tempted to touch her. But the moment the lady turned her back towards Enrique, he was surprised once again. She had a small but clearly visible tattoo. Was she a member of the Yakuza? He didn't think there were any female Yakuza members. Was it just a dream?

Sweet smells

A little bored because Clara wasn't at school today, Tim spent the break alone on the bench. With spring in full swing, the air was fresh and clear. Though still a little chilly, Tim enjoyed being able to breathe properly again. Just a few days ago his nose was still blocked from a cold, but now he could smell again. This was something that excited him, even though he still wondered how he could remember and distinguish all the different smells that his nose was tickled with. Certainly he knew when his mum was cooking his favourite dish, because as soon as he got home and dropped his school bag, his nose knew exactly what would be on the plate later on.

Tim had just finished his snack when his nose captured a sweet ripe smell, something like a mix of berries, maybe more strawberries than other berries. What a tempting smell. Turning around, Tim tried to figure out where it was coming from. Then he realized that his classmate sitting on the other bench had just peeled a very ripe banana. Even across the short distance he could smell it. A little disappointed that his nose had been misled by the mix of olfactory molecules, Tim decided that he wanted to ask his science teacher how humans were able to remember smells. Did our brain store a file card with a kind of fingerprint of each of the smells we came across? Tim was sure that he would always remember certain smells, like for example the one in the circus. But even if we have file card storage to keep track of what olfactory mixes tickle our nostrils, how do we decide which smells appeal or don't appeal to us? There must be something that tells us, though Tim didn't know what. Something must be guiding us through the jungle of smells and odours. Tim imagined that it would work in a similar way as the smell of flowers, which attracts bees.

No smell, but the bell caught Tim's attention next. Time to go back to class.

Up in the Sky

Cassiopeia needed some fresh air for her mind. She needed to clear all her thoughts and take a deep breath in order to feel light again. Too many thoughts were occupying her and sticking around. The easiest way for her to calm her grey matter was to find a cosy piece of green in the park, put her navy blue sling-back under her head and watch the sky. Her eyes would follow all those fluffy pieces of cotton passing by until she fell asleep or ended up in a state of complete relaxation.

In her imagination she took all the things that occupied her mind piece by piece and attached them to a piece of sky cotton. Some of the thoughts were heavy and she needed to tie them tightly to the cloud that was carrying them away. Other thoughts were light and she could just pin them there. For some she needed imaginary glue.

To Cassiopeia clouds were as delicate as the thoughts that surrounded and occupied us. Some of them were meant to stay, while others were meant to fade away.

Looking at the constant transformation of the clouds from below, with her head in the clouds, Cassiopeia reminded herself how the world around us is constantly being re-created by what we want to see. Never should we give in to thoughts that are weighing too heavy on us and preventing us from taking off to the sky!

SPEED-CLOCK

Tim's mum was upset today. She had received a photo from the police and Tim wondered why. When he enquired he got a grumpy "I-drove-too-fast-and-now-I-have-to-pay-a-fine" as an answer. It was something that Tim didn't understand, the thing about the photo and the thing about the fine.

But there was this matter that he had been wondering about for quite some time. He knew that in the car there was an indicator that displayed the speed in numbers. He always observed it from the backseat whenever his mum or dad was driving. But which device did humans possess to gauge speed? How do we know what is fast and what is slow? Are we too fast when we become dizzy due to the acceleration? Are we too slow when our friends get impatient?

The other day when Tim was cycling around the block, his mum screamed after him "don't ride too fast Tim!" He wondered why she made such a fuss as he was enjoying the light breeze from the ride and didn't feel he was cycling fast, it was just right. It must be that humans had different types of speed clocks and that was why there was this confusion with the police!

JOY RIDE

What a day. Mana hadn't felt like this for a long time. Having left the office early today, she'd just finished running and was lying on the bench in the park. A little exhausted but filled with a contented feeling of happiness caused by the body's release of endorphins, she was staring at the stale blue sky.

With her eyes closed, Mana paid close attention to the noises around her. Hearing herself breathe, people walking past and the birds having lively discussions, she was sure that she had a big smile on her face.

Somehow, ever since getting up this morning, she felt energized and riding on the top of her mood curve. Nothing seemed impossible today, which was totally contrary to other days when she would usually be fully occupied by her own thoughts and worries going round in circles. Though she had had a busy and pretty hectic day in the office, she was confident in handling all the matters brought to her attention and was even complemented for her professionalism and expertise by her co-workers.

Resting in the park as the day seemed to have just started even though she had already spent a full day at work, Mana felt as if she could breathe in the energy of the intense colours of spring, with beautiful flowers contrasting with the lush green of the grass and everything appearing so pure and novel.

Maybe her excitement also had another cause. She had a rare dinner date with a new friend later on. She had seen him a few times but finally caught his attention and was invited for dinner. Mana was utterly excited about her new encounter and wasn't quite sure yet how to fit it into her life.

As the effect of the endorphins subsided a little bit, Mana found that it was time to go home and prepare for the night. On the way home she also wanted to make a short stop at her usual place for prayers and express her wishes to the deities of the temple.

ON THE SURFACE

It was exam time and Cassiopeia was glad the day was over. Her tension began to subside as she handed in her paper and relief settled in. As she left the exam hall Cassiopeia found one of her course mates sitting on the floor in the corridor, crying and breathing heavily. Breathing quickly and sobbing at the same time, she expressed her devastation about the exam. Cassiopeia tried to calm her down but realized that her course mate was close to hyperventilating. She took her hands and placed them on her tummy and asked her to pause between breathing in and out. After some time she finally seemed to calm down a little bit. Cassiopeia was still confused by what she had witnessed though it didn't come as a surprise because her Yoga teacher in Nepal had made her aware of that fact before. Most people breathe shallowly.

With our upbringing we seem to lose the ability to breathe deeply like babies do. Losing this ability, we jeopardize our energetic well-being and access to what some call the true self. Only through regular practise can we maintain our balance. Taking a deep breath, Cassiopeia left the campus.

FRAGILE MEMORIES

It was Saturday just before noon and Tim was about to meet Clara in the playground. He was sitting on the bench, watching the other kids play.

Last night Tim had a very exciting dream and he wanted to tell Clara all about it. He was an engine driver of a steam engine. He couldn't remember exactly where he had started his journey but the landscapes that he passed seemed like postcards to him. Be it tracks close to a river where Tim was stunned by the intense green of the grass left and right as he looked out from his driver's cab, or when crossing a deep gorge high up on a century old viaduct. He felt like he was driving through a model railway landscape and all that he could see was perfectly arranged. What excited him most was when his steam engine entered a tunnel. Since he wasn't familiar with the track, whatever was waiting on the other side of the tunnel was always a pleasant surprise. He could even smell the coal during his dream.

Tim? Tim? Oh, Clara! Tim was so absorbed in replaying the vivid images that he remembered from his dream that he hadn't even realized Clara had arrived in the meantime. Tim immediately wanted to tell Clara about his fascinating dream but the moment he came back to reality his dream was gone in a split second. How could that be? He knew what he had dreamt but he just couldn't remember any of the rich postcard pictures let alone describe them to Clara who was standing in front of him waiting to play. Not knowing why we sometimes remember a dream for a long time and other times it's gone, just blown away within a wink, was a mystery to Tim.

But now Clara was getting impatient and she asked him to join her on the swing.

GLASS MARBLES

It was time to study, time to prepare for her last round of exams at the end of spring. Cassiopeia was sitting at her desk at home and tried to get herself into the mood to study but she found it hard to concentrate and stay focussed. Her mind was constantly straying. The weather was kind of gloomy, which one would think was ideal for exam preparation but to Cassiopeia it was the type of weather that put her in a philosophical mood.

As it started raining Cassiopeia still couldn't focus on preparing for her exams. Rather, she started looking outside and observed how the raindrops were hitting the windows. As the rain intensified Cassiopeia's nose was no longer pointing at any of the books on her desk but was nearly glued to the large balcony window in her room. From the closest possible distance she was studying the fine water drops lined up on the window's surface.

Somehow these pearls of water looked like glass marbles to Cassiopeia. Glass marbles like the ones she collected when she was younger. At that time she spent hours gazing through the glass marbles while holding them towards a source of light. Now, grown up, she no longer collected glass marbles but still enjoyed looking at them in the jar on her bookshelf.

Like the water drops on the surface of her window, glass marbles would magnify things, blur the view or put things into a different perspective depending on their unique characteristics. What if each of us was given a virgin glass marble upon arrival on planet Earth? Our task would be to record our lives by painting the marble in our own unique way as we move along our paths and grow. What kind of colours from all the marbles would we get to see once light or sunrays hit them? Certainly a stunning diversity of different colours and shades provided we dare to stain the blank page in a bid to produce a truly inimitable piece of art.

Stars of the Economy

When Marc appeared in his client's office early that morning he was confronted with an atmosphere characterised by a lack of understanding, paralysis and grief. Never in his young professional career to date had he experienced such moving encounters with employees and the moment one of his colleagues told him the related news Marc felt odd and lost.

Apparently the CEO of his client's company had been found dead the night before and though the cause of death was still subject to further investigation, rumours were spreading that it was suicide.

A recognized leader, valued professional and proud dad chose the golden shot over the golden parachute in a desperate attempt to escape a system which does not permit slowdowns or accept failure. An environment where healthy employees turn into amphetamine addicted robots trying to cope with what irrational markets demand from human beings like they do from machines following the premise that there was always a way to achieve more, regardless of the consequences and sustainability. What was imaginable in the digital world where acceleration was a matter of algorithms was equally applied to people, even though it contradicted the nature of human beings.

Shocked that what Marc knew from occasional news about fame-deprived music- or film-stars has now become reality in an environment where he thought he was going to earn his living for the next 30 years, made him deeply concerned. How could he contribute to a change? Which paradigm should he question? The work ahead seemed impossible with all this confusion weighing down on Marc's shoulders.

MASQUERADE

Cassiopeia was on her way to university. For one of her papers she had to do some research in the library. Approaching the campus, she was surprised to see the large crowds surrounding the main hall on the campus. She didn't usually have classes on Wednesday; therefore she wasn't quite sure what was going on. Only a few moments later she caught a glimpse of the promotional flags surrounding the building. It was the middle of May and time for the career fair!

Time for the annual masquerade, which reminded Cassiopeia of a parade of penguins. Everyone was dressed in black and white as if they were the only two colours in the world. As she walked to the library building, she occasionally managed to spot some brave dots of colour in the crowd but those people must have felt like aliens among all the uniformed graduates from the same mould. But they weren't! Why was there this full conformity in such a completely individualistic society? Misled by clothes, we seem tempted to think we can only play the game if we abide by the rules of the fashion of the trade. Was it our hardwired biological predisposition ensuring our survival, which deceived our brain as our sight always took priority? From her reading of neuroscience magazines, Cassiopeia knew that even wine connoisseurs were prone to mistakes if the colour of the wine was manipulated. But how could we escape from being uncritically trapped by the first impression? From what we see? It seemed like a work-load optimizing short-cut performed by our brain to judge things by the cover. Something that could only lead to trouble and disappointment once the masks were off and the truth revealed. This wasn't what she wanted. Cassiopeia didn't want to be disappointed, she wanted to embrace diversity and cultivate her curiosity. Time to practice mindfulness Cassiopeia.

DISCOVERY CHANNEL

Tim was a little upset. He was excitedly telling his dad about one of the first novels that he had started reading earlier that day. It was about some of the greatest ancient adventurers and their remarkably brave journeys. He was fascinated by their spirit and courage; facing uncertainty, they must have eagerly waited for rewarding moments of discovery. Tim instantly started to picture himself with some of his friends on such a rewarding expedition. They would start at the end of the world, in Ushuaia, to find out what was going to come after the end.

And all his dad said was, well, if you want to do that, then you need to be well prepared! What is there to be discovered if we need to be prepared for everything? Hmm, sometimes he wondered what could still be discovered anyway. It seemed that for all his questions, his teachers, friends and family always already had the answers ready. Detailed maps existed for all the places in the world, so where could he find a white undiscovered part on the globe?

But then, on the spur of the moment, Tim remembered another conversation he'd had with his dad. The other day he was scrutinizing the way we dream and why dreams occur while we sleep. It seemed that his dad didn't have as many answers in this domain. Why can some people remember their dreams clearly and others can't? Why do we dream while we are asleep? Do animals also dream?

Maybe that could be Tim's spot on the map of discoveries? His enthusiasm suddenly returned. Being a scientist and figuring out how our dreams fit into the big picture would go well with his aspiration to become a dream writer! Tomorrow he would have to convince Clara to volunteer one more time as a guinea pig for his studies!

ACCELERATING EXPRESSION

Cassiopeia had finished her classes and was off into town. She wanted to drop by one of her favourite stores, an old-fashioned paper manufacturer and print shop. She loved the crowded shop with its manufacturing facilities at the back of the building. Whenever she entered the shop the air was filled with a mix of somehow sweet smells of paper, printing ink and lubricating grease. Cassiopeia was fond of this craft, which produced beautiful cards, calendars and books of all kinds. Her handwritten diary, for which she used a book from this shop, was her most precious treasure.

Writing her papers at university, Cassiopeia realized her adversity to keyboards. Typing on a keyboard seemed to coincide with acceleration. It didn't leave much room for pauses or reflections. It made everything look so uniform. But humans are not alike and don't operate at a uniform processing speed like CPUs, our brains adapt to what is required and some ideas, thoughts and emotions need time to ripen before they build up or can be expressed. Handwriting allows us to sketch them first and complete them later, while typing on a keyboard somehow tempts us to complete the process quicker, bearing in mind that typed words can always be rephrased, amended or erased.

Maybe there were positive sides to it too, but having seen the younger generations which seem to have lost their ability to handwrite, Cassiopeia felt once more that distinctions are traded for homogeneity as evolution progresses.

II

Though the tree provided shade, the temperature was rising and the heat of the surrounding land was prickling. There was another person around. Though somehow familiar to the group, there was this feeling of foreignness and novelty in the air. Considering the heat, one could have been tempted to believe that it was a fata morgana. But it wasn't. It was something new emerging. Something strongly rooted and with a firm place waiting to be discovered more and more.

SUMMER

TRAIN-ING THE WORLD

Tim was off to his dreams again. But this time with questions in his mind. For decades rail-tracks have covered the globe. So have locomotives and trains, which were placed on those tracks all over the world. Would the locomotives be locked and if yes, who would have the keys and where would they be kept? In central train stations? In the station master's house? Tim was imagining a big wooden board hanging somewhere on the wall, with a set of keys hanging on each carefully numbered hook representing a locomotive. If it were for him to decide, Tim would create a global key that was suitable for all locomotives.

Picturing himself as an engine driver in the driver's cabin, Tim wondered what would entitle him to train the world. Would he have to go to school first and learn all the subjects before he could set off to discover the world off the tracks? It didn't matter for now; he was already in his imaginary locomotive, tasting the smell of oil-lubricated metal, the running engine and a breeze of adventure. Enjoying the quietness of the driver's cabin and listening to the monotonous tatata tatata tatata produced by the steel wheels on the tracks, his eyes were busy watching the movie presented through the windows surrounding him. The speed was just right to keep him curious, and at times he was astonished and overwhelmed. Not too fast like on a flight, not too slow as when on foot. For a while he was cruising through luscious green paddy fields with farmers standing in light muddy water up to their knees, wearing cone shaped hats, moving their bodies up and down, plucking the rice. At one point he caught sight of a pagoda and shortly thereafter a bunch of novices in their distinct orange coloured cowls obviously on their way to the temple. Then again, his locomotive would work its way up to the top of snow-covered mountains, first through cooling conifer forests, then crossing gorges across ancient stone viaducts and finally entering tunnels just to anticipate the sun at the other end. Not much after, Tim's face would be glued to the window as he was amazed by the endless steppe in Namibia, which seemed to be on fire judging by the colours produced by the sunset. Herds of zebras, elephants and antelopes would appear one by one, almost like in the neatly arranged zoo at home.

As his journey continued Tim wondered how he would find his way around the globe. Would he need a map? Should he just follow the tracks? How would he deal with all the differences? Gauge, voltage, traffic rules...and there it was, the signal of the arriving train, time to get up and ready for school Tim!

DERAILED BY EXPECTATIONS

What a day. Stopping at the usual place on her way home, Mana was still trying to cope with the happenings of the day. Just two years after graduating from the leading business school and starting her job as a junior accountant, she was unexpectedly promoted to senior accountant with immediate effect. At least it was sudden for her, though all her colleagues insisted during the celebrations at lunch that it wasn't a surprise as their boss always praised her for being a bright employee with extraordinary diligence and dedication. But Mana didn't feel excited about her promotion at all. Realizing the expectations placed on her, she felt like an extra load was being put on her shoulders. Her parents were so proud when their daughter graduated with flying colours two years ago, and they would certainly be delighted to hear that she had already been promoted at such an early stage in her career. So how could she possibly go home and tell her parents that she wanted to do something totally different in life and not what she was doing right now?

Just because she was intelligent and a hard worker it didn't mean she enjoyed being an accountant and that her work brought her satisfaction. More likely it ate up all the energy that she wanted to invest in pursuing her dreams.

Quiet as she was, Mana didn't really blame her parents, but how could the people around her possibly know her own vision for her life? A vision which would be the driving force propelling her forward without the struggle of getting up early in the morning and dragging herself to work every day.

Mana had various dreams about what she wanted to do with her life, but she was afraid to say them out loud. For most of her life she grew up fulfilling the expectations of her social environment, most prominently of course her parents' expectations, so how could she possibly disappoint them now? But she felt increasingly reluctant to live up to any expectations other than her own; whose life was it anyway?

FADING SMILES

With the wind blowing her curly hair, Cassiopeia was enjoying the intense blue of the lake in front of her. She had just returned from two months abroad and was holding her sunshade pendant in her hand where the Henna drawings were slowly fading. While she physically arrived a day ago, she was still in a mental state of transmission, longing for the spiritual environment and the hospitality of her host family.

Cassiopeia was in Nepal for two months. It filled her with utmost satisfaction to teach her slightly younger female counterparts English as they were often at a disadvantage compared to boys who would get to go to school first if the family's funds were limited. Cassiopeia was astounded by the sensitivity of her Nepali hosts. On the day of her departure she went to her favourite Buddhist temple for the last time, lit the joss sticks as she had been taught by the younger sister in the host family, and then took a seat to absorb the peacefulness of her surroundings. It was then that an elderly Nepali asked her in nearly fluent English why she was sad. Well, Cassiopeia hadn't told anyone that she was sad to be leaving, but it wasn't the first time that she was surprised by what people here seemed to perceive, while in her homeland people no longer seemed to possess those skills.

And that's why she was sitting here, staring into the bright day. Though excited to be travelling back home and to see her family, she was surprised to realise that the smile on people's faces seemed to gradually disappear the further West she travelled. Why she wondered, would people who live off a small amount of income, and face the dilemma of choosing one of their three children to send to school because sending all three would be beyond the family's means, be carrying a smile on their face at any time of the day? Most likely even while sleeping. Was it the material wealth and constantly striving for more of the people in her homeland that was traded for the smile on their faces? Was it because they were preoccupied with choosing the right probiotic yoghurt that was the best for their colon instead of nurturing themselves spiritually?

MOULDS THAT SHAPE US

Talking about their son- and daughter-in-law, Ruth and Walter realized how much the environment we grow up in plays a role in who we actually become later in life.

For example, Céline, their daughter-in-law, grew up as the daughter of an air force pilot and lived most of the first part of her life near an army base. In an environment dominated by men, her interest in technical stuff and engineering was cultivated. Gifted in this interest, she is now leading a small group of development engineers in a medium-sized firm without an engineering degree but instead has a solid business background.

Or Paul, their son-in-law, who never tires of mentioning how unfairly he was treated by his parents compared to his siblings and today is an excellent lawyer with an incredibly strong sense of justice.

The same is true for Susan, their daughter's best friend. Growing up in a relatively poor family, Susan had to manage her finances from an early age. Just out from school and wanting to study at university, she had to fund her living expenses and study fees herself after her father's sudden death. She worked part-time and managed to complete her degree within the usual time. Not surprisingly she developed a strong interest in financial matters and ended up graduating with a degree in accounting and finance. The unexpected and sudden loss of her dad at an early age rattled Susan's view of life. Ever since she has spent her time organising every part of her life, from cleaning the house, meeting friends, scheduling sessions to study, allocating time for sports and even dating. It seems like she has banned spontaneity from her life with a strict regime of tasks filling day after day, as if she wants to make sure that any further uncertainty in life and with it any other rattling surprise are avoided.

On his recent trip to Singapore with a group of friends, Walter was once more reminded of the important role teachers can play in who we become. While waiting for his sushi dishes to be prepared he observed how the apprentice who was a foreign national was being bullied by his boss and master with silly tasks. This was not to make him learn but to unnecessarily clarify who is in charge. A good teacher would have been more mature than this one was. Much to Walter's disliking he seemed to be doing his utmost to discourage a young and curious student from becoming a bright chef one day by heavily jeopardizing his pupil's self-confidence.

IN SEARCH OF A GEM

It was unusual for Mana to be out alone that late at night but she just needed to breathe. Though it was too late to go to her favourite spot in the park, she managed to find a place near her house where she could be on her own for a while. Her parents were excited when she told them about her unexpected promotion the other day. But Mana wasn't. And though she was gathering more and more courage to liberate herself from the expectations placed on her by others, she didn't yet know how she could possibly pursue her dream.

Mana's father was a well-recognized goldsmith in Tokyo. Upon retiring he sold his business to his only employee who had worked with him for a long time. Though business was going well and he certainly gained lots of satisfaction from his work while he was still actively involved, he always insisted that Mana would learn something proper and not follow in his footsteps. Accommodating, as Mana was, she was never opposed her father's wish even though at times she wasn't sure whether studying accounting would be the right thing to do. Now, when everyone was celebrating her promotion, Mana felt at odds with herself.

Having spent many hours of her childhood in her father's workshop, Mana had always been fascinated by the gems her father used in his crafts. The intense colours nature produced in the shape of blue sapphires, red rubies, green emeralds and purple amethysts was something that left a magic spell on her. She wasn't specifically interested in diamonds but more so in all the other less common gems. She never paid much attention to this particular interest, which has been lurking in her ever since she was a child. But this time she wasn't able to brush her fascination aside. Somehow it gave her strength and caused her to worry at the same time.

It seemed that her vision of what she wanted to pursue in her life had gradually become clearer but was yet far from being ripe for a decision. Mana knew what she wanted to do for the rest of her life but she had yet to gain clarity about how to do it. Maybe because her aspiration sounded a little funny to others, especially considering her reserved and shy nature. But there was no doubt about its meaningfulness to her. Mana wanted to be a professional gem hunter. She didn't know entirely what would qualify her for this except for her fascination, dedication and persistence in whatever she had done in the past as well as her analytical skills which she thought would be useful when assessing hints on where rare gem stones could be found. She knew she wasn't particularly adventurous, but for matters of such personal importance she was willing to take certain risks. She wasn't afraid to get her hands dirty with mud, searching the promising mining sites in the hope of eventually being rewarded with the discovery of a luminous gem. Like in her current job as an accountant, where she appeared to be very professional and confident, Mana was sure she would excel as a gem hunter once she acquired sufficient knowledge and gained some experience.

Lost in her thoughts, Mana realized that her aspiration to become a professional gem hunter might have something in common with another domain in her life. Finding someone she could share her life with was like starting off on a hunt for a rare gem. Not an easy though certainly meaningful journey, but one that might require both courage and wisdom at times. Once they had found each other they could create a beautiful piece of craft together by refining the unique traits of the gem. Glad to have spent some time reflecting on her own, Mana decided to head home, her face decorated with an attractive smile.

HEADS DOWN

Cassiopeia and Celia were having their lunch in the university park. Cassiopeia usually brought a sandwich from home. After an exhausting morning full of lectures, they were both in need of fresh air and some food first. Enjoying the crispy home-baked bread with alternate layers of ham, Swiss cheese and gherkins, Cassiopeia observed Celia who was sitting with her on the bench but also the other students spread all over the park.

Barely any of her fellow students were sitting upright, and instead of looking straight ahead or being engaged in lively discussions, most had their heads down. It wasn't because their heads felt heavy due to all the newly acquired knowledge. They weren't paying respect by bending their heads either, as students from other countries would. Neither were they sad or in mourning.

Cassiopeia realized that all the heads were facing a little screen, usually held in the palm of one hand, while multi-tasking the food supply towards their mouths with the remaining five fingers of the other hand. The majority of her classmates, seniors and juniors were busy using their smartphones in order to stay connected with the world, not realizing that they barely looked at their neighbours during lunch anymore.

The entire atmosphere seemed to have an impersonal touch. Cassiopeia's mind prompted her to ask lots of questions. How could we possibly transmit the wealth of implicit and explicit messages usually exchanged via glances or conversations facing each other with a limited range of letters and emoticons to communicate our state of mind or intimate emotions?

Our eyes are our window to the world, our individual perception shaping the way we view reality. But for Cassiopeia, the eyes were also mirrors. Unbiased mirrors which give us an uncountable number of hints on how our counterparts see the world or us. With our heads always facing down, Cassiopeia wondered how many of us were still able to remember the colour of the eyes in the mirror opposite us. Would we still be able to tell whether eyes wide open revealing the entirety of the pupils signalled excitement, pain, joy or fear?

The loss of such ability appeared irreplaceable to Cassiopeia and she was glad that Celia had brought her attention back to the delicious sandwich before she could dwell on her thoughts any longer.

MESSAGE IN A BOTTLE

It was one of those beautiful summer days, not too hot, not too cold, with a nice warm breeze and blue skies. Tim wanted to enjoy his free afternoon playing in his parents' garden but first he had to help his mum in the kitchen. He didn't mind, in fact he loved those moments when the air in the kitchen was filled with flavours and fragrances of all kinds. He was tasked with slicing the stunningly yellow and slightly rosy apricots so they could be soaked in sugar before being cooked in the gigantic copper pan. He was completely absorbed by the sweet smell of the fruits and the crystallizing sugar as his mum was making the jam. The entire kitchen counter was full with freshly washed empty preserving jars, which were waiting to be filled...

And off he was. Waiting for the jam to be ready for bottling, Tim started daydreaming. He imagined himself in one of those jars. The lid of the jar was the hatch of his imaginary ship. He was riding the waves, manoeuvring between icebergs, rubbing the glass as it fogged up in tropical waters. The transparency of the glass jar provided him with sunlight, allowed him to observe the stars at night, magnified the beautiful fishes surrounding him during his journey, super sized the already big container vessels crossing the oceans and made strange sounds when floating rubbish hit it from the side. Though a little turbulent at times, Tim felt comfortable in his tiny vacuum sealed jar. Occasionally, he longed for some fresh air and he tried to open the lid of his fictitious ship a little bit to catch some of the salty sea breeze. No noise from radio communication, only the sound of the waves and his own breath could be heard. Which route should he take? Where would the bottle take him? Tim wasn't worried because somehow an unknown confidence comforted him that luck and faith would take him around the world and things would turn out well. He only had one wish, to run ashore eventually, only to be picked up by Clara who would wake him up from his dream.

IN SEARCH OF LIGHT

Mana was indulging in reminiscences. She loved the summer days at her grandparents' house in the countryside where she used to spend her summer holidays when she was a kid.

The house was mainly made of wood and was situated in a quiet area at the end of a tiny village about four and a half hours outside Tokyo. As Mana grew older she learnt to appreciate the peacefulness and the simplicity of her grandparents' lifestyle in the countryside. Whenever she longed for a break from the city's hustle and bustle she recalled the moments that she had enjoyed with them. Mana had loved to read ever since she was small and received her first book. While at her grandparents' house she developed a habit. Even during the summer holidays her grandma, who was concerned about her granddaughter's timely and sufficient rest, would switch off all the lights in the house by eight at the latest. While her grandparents sat outside next to each other, watching the arrival of the night in the presence of a flickering candle, often without speaking a word, the expectation was that

Mana would be asleep in her bed. Mana loved to peak at her grandparents from her room. She was fascinated by the shadows playing hide and seek as the flame of the candle danced lightly with each blow of warm summer wind.

During the day Mana would spend hours in the garden with her grandparents and sat comfortably in the shade of the wooden house reading one of her many books that she brought with her when she went for her holiday. But every night, as her grandma insisted that it was time to sleep, Mana went off in search of some light. With many of her books too interesting to be kept unread until the next day, she would make use of the house's old construction style which left some gaps between the dark wooden planks and the sliding doors. Moving around in her room to find the best spot to catch some of the remaining daylight from outside, Mana would sit close to the walls and windows in order to continue reading for as long as possible. Only when her eyelids were too tired and she started to close them frequently as she attempted to read the same page again and again, she would get ready for bed, usually falling asleep instantly full of satisfaction and totally immersed in the story she had just read, forgetting about her surroundings and ending with a deep, peaceful sleep until she was awoken by the neighbour's cockerel the following morning.

TWINKLING MEMORIES

Somnolent as Cassiopeia was, she decided to go for a walk. It was just after midnight but somehow her mind didn't want to rest. Instead of turning constantly in her bed she preferred to get some air, walking for a while and enjoying some quiet moments at her favourite spot near the river. The air was a little cool but very refreshing, just what she needed. She took a seat on the bench near the river, lifted her head up and looked at the sky.

Only then did she realize how clear the night was. Pitch black, yet creating an infinite space of unknown dimensions, the dark of the night seemed to be a perfect match for the twinkling sources of light forming the different constellations of the stars in the sky. Cassiopeia had never asked her parents why they chose the name she carried today. She knew little about the origins of her name except that it was easily recognizable in the sky due to its prominent 'W' shape and that the constellation was named after a queen in Greek mythology.

Considered to be some of the most luminous stars around, Cassiopeia could see herself in the sky tonight. The serenity of the night calmed and inspired Cassiopeia at the same time.

How would she explain the happenings in the sky to a five year old if she were asked? She found that her own figurative explanation, which she made up during another restless night quite some time ago, might be the most suitable one.

For Cassiopeia the night sky was like a map of memories. Each star represented a memorable moment. New memories might be more salient or luminous on a clear night. Some stars might twinkle more than others. Some stars, like memories, would fade over time; become less bright and even disappear into the infinite black once nature's cycle came to an end. Some stars might only be visible on certain nights, like memories that we only recall under certain circumstances. And other stars will always appear firmly visible every night, guiding us on our paths like lighthouses, which remind us of the surrounding land. As such, the night sky, a piece of black velvet covered with diamond dust, was a map of memories which helped Cassiopeia to recall memorable moments which gave and still give her guidance in her life. Right now, with all that she had learnt, the memory of her recent volunteer stay in Nepal was definitely the most luminous star in her sky.

While the sky was the same for everyone, everyone looked at it from a different angle and filled it with his or her own memorable moments. Time to sleep Cassiopeia.

TENDERNESS

Mana was breathing heavily. Not out of fear but joy. Paolo was lying beside her, drifting off to a satisfied sleep. They were in Paolo's cosy apartment above his shop. Mana was too awake to sleep, as images and scenes from the day and the last moments appeared in front of her randomly and at lightning speed. It all seemed unreal.

She remembered Paolo's gentle strokes on her body as they were about to sleep. Hesitating first she gradually couldn't resist her increasing desire. At the very same moment, she felt an urge to hide her face. The darkness of the room offered her the much-wanted cover. A current was flowing between them and encouraged by Paolo's subtle touches, she joined the bodily discovery tour in the middle of the night. As they mapped each other's bodies with bare hands, she remembered each dimple, mole and scar, and his skin was smooth and soft like just after having a shower. As the ecstasy increased their bodies became warm and blood rushed through each and every cell. It was Mana's first intense moment of intimacy. Her first night out.

She was struggling to balance her socialized shyness and the brute desire. It was like a disputation between deeply rooted biological desires and the conscious mind. Sexual attraction was something new to her and she was very thankful for Paolo's unconditional understanding. Giving in to the flow didn't require as much courage as she had thought. Her body was filled with warmth. She felt safe and protected. In her slumberous state of mind tiny tears started rolling down her face. Happiness was overwhelming.

THE SIZE OF BITES

Tim was resting in the garden after finishing his lunch. He was off school that afternoon. Before getting his homework done he wanted to enjoy the sun for a while. Yesterday he didn't eat lunch at home as he usually did because his mum had to work a little longer. Instead, he went to his best friend's house.

He realized that the younger sister of his friend was eating with a smaller set of cutlery than he and his friend were. Why would children use small forks and spoons? Growing up, they were in need of lots of nutrients, so carrying all that into their hungry mouths wouldn't it be more sensible to have a big fork and spoon?

He decided to ask his mum later on; though he was pretty sure she would say a big fork and spoon would be too heavy or dangerous for kids to use.

Hmm. Tim was still brooding about the size of things on the dining table. His dad was always the first to finish his meals when they were eating and Tim recalled his mum repeatedly telling his dad to eat slower. Again and again she reminded him that food was there to be appreciated and enjoyed because not everybody has the privilege to eat three meals a day. Tim knew little about kids who had to go to school without breakfast because there wasn't enough money in the family to buy food, something that his mum always mentioned to him when he didn't finish his meal. But he didn't quite understand what she meant by appreciating the dishes that she cooked.

Did she just want his dad to eat slower? Would it work if his dad had to use a smaller fork and spoon?

Tim thought that eating smaller mouthfuls at a time should make him slow down. He decided to try. Tonight, when his mum wanted him to set the table for dinner he would choose the small set of cutlery for his dad, which he used before he went to nursery. He was curious to see what his dad would say. He just would have to make sure he was sitting at the table before his dad, otherwise he would definitely sit in Tim's place where he would have placed the big fork and spoon, because he was still growing and he needed to eat a lot.

SHOWTIME!

Cassiopeia was attending a friend's wedding. It was one of the first wedding invitations that she had received for a long time, at least in this part of the world. But she was utterly disappointed by how this occasion was celebrated. It seemed that this important tradition in a couple's life has just become yet another commercial event instead of a moment in time which served the good of the society and fostered a bond among people. While she was in Nepal she had the rare opportunity to witness a Nepali wedding ceremony, which lasted nearly three days. It was far from being commercialized; rather it was a ritual that moved Cassiopeia more than she had ever experienced before. It was an occasion where neighbours and entire communities gathered to celebrate this lifetime event of the two families.

Another deeply moving experience was a ritual in Tibet, which she witnessed during her stay there. It served to calm the mountain gods and reminded all the participants of their intimate relationship with their environment and that they were an integral part of nature.

Why was it that all those rituals and traditions seemed to have lost their stand in the developed world? Traditions that have been conserved for centuries that are gradually being phased out like an outdated product. Yet, it appeared to Cassiopeia that there wasn't a replacement that was on a par with what had been lost. Where did today's citizens of the world learn their beliefs? Find consolation for their losses? Cheer out of joy? Treasure moments of unconditional familiarity with their loved ones? It seems that when humans still feared demons they trusted rituals to console the demons and to protect themselves from bad luck. Now it was left to the insurance business to comfort the world's citizens who have lost their spiritual roots.

LIVING IN AN IMPERFECT WORLD

Ruth had just come back from shopping with her best school friend from her younger days. They always met on and off for some activity. While they were having a coffee together Ruth complained about Walter. Again, she had had to buy flowers for herself, as after 56 years of marriage Walter didn't even buy flowers for her occasionally. At times upset about it, Ruth needed to vent her anger by complaining to Esther.

It was the same for her interest in astrology. This is one of the subjects she would never get to have a constructive discussion with Walter about. While he was interested in the happenings in the sky and was active in the local astronomy association, where he gave tours to visitors on a voluntary basis at the observatory. But Walter never even wanted to try to understand how much of the happenings in our daily lives are in fact influenced by astrological constellations, as Ruth had discovered in the last two years by attending seminars and conferences on that matter.

While she recognized that Walter was getting tired of her astrological explanations for the world's affairs, she was sure he still loved her the same as he did when they first met and a spark ignited a feeling that had lasted ever since.

Though they frequently argued, like sudden downpours and storms in summer, the air was always clear thereafter and things were back in place for both of them. This was something Ruth didn't see much anymore with the youngsters. They seemed to be in trouble living in an imperfect world. She found that those who grew up comfortably with all the benefits of the wealth that had been created by previous generations take many things for granted and are not grateful for all the opportunities to hand, while at the same time struggle to find their place in an ever-changing world. Esther wanted to leave so Ruth stopped grumbling about today's youth.

Parting

Mana was on the way to the airport with Paolo. One of his close cousins had died unexpectedly in an accident. Usually Mana associated positive feelings about going to the airport, either out of excitement because the holiday was impending or joy because it meant she could welcome home one of her loved ones.

But this time her feelings were mixed. She did not know whether to feel despair or relief about this sudden break. She was a thorn between her intense attraction to Paolo and the moments of distance.

Do we ever learn to part, even if it is just temporary? It was the hardest thing in life and something that couldn't be taught at school. Why do we struggle so much? Because we forget to live in the moment?

Mana didn't have the answers. All she knew was that she had rarely experienced such strong emotions. Emotions that made her feel alive. Was this a real taste of life?

LIGHTS ON!

Tim caught a glimpse of some disturbing images today before heading to bed when his parents were watching the news. Though he didn't the see details while peaking from the corridor, he saw what they called war. It looked like a firework, but not one in bright colours that made people go ah..oh..ah.., rather the opposite. It terrified them, left them running for shelter while screaming for their life. The constant rattling of bombs and guns produced a deafening noise. Buildings gave way to the destroying forces and wounded people collapsed.

What a mess it was. It looked awful and Tim was sure that no human being would survive for long under such circumstances. Tim couldn't think of any reason anyone would want such a situation to persist.

Like for his room, he was convinced that a minimal level of order had to be maintained. Maybe human beings had to be forced to get things in order. Tim thought of ways how to do that. How about leaving the light on? If there wasn't a night there wouldn't be a break. Humans would have to face the mess and clean it up as soon as possible. If things weren't resolved, he wouldn't let them sleep. With the brightness of the day leaving no dark spots to hide, they would have to work together to get things in order. If he didn't clean his room and put his toys away, his parents wouldn't let Tim move on to more enjoyable activities. Somehow a little order seemed necessary for the world to function. Would they all understand what needed to be done if the light was on for days?

Tim wasn't sure as he headed to bed. The images, which continued to appear in front of his eyes, were still incomprehensible to him, but that's maybe why his parents didn't let him watch the evening news yet. With his room in order and the warmth and comfort of his bed, Tim was lucky to be off to dreamland quickly, not being kept awake by memories of the ugly side of the world.

SUSTAINABLE FOUNDATION?

Ruth told Walter about the discussion with Esther the other day. Of course she wouldn't mention her dissatisfaction about the flowers, but they were talking about the wealth that might have spoiled the younger generation. For Walter the wealth itself wasn't the issue, he was more concerned about the foundations of it in the industrialized and developed nations today. Debt-loaded nations, which emerged as highly developed states with a comfortable per capita income based on propagated free markets, which all of a sudden seemed to be on the brink of collapse. Were the economic models and assumptions that formed the foundations of the wealth enjoyed by younger generations today really sustainable? If not, would those who grew up spoiled with choice, yet still indecisive, be in a position to change the way forward?

FRAMING THE MOMENT

Cassiopeia was sitting on the window ledge in her room. The air loaded with water drops and moisture just after a heavy summer downpour, she was contemplating the world as she liked to do. Cassiopeia was paying close attention to the subtle changes of colours as the night was setting in. It seemed like Zeus was playing with his indefinite palette of soothing pastel colours. From baby blue to mauve, with the occasional strokes of pink and gold, nature seemed to have a secret formula for colour harmony. The breath-taking colours of the sky made Cassiopeia feel that she wanted to hold on to the beautiful sight as long as possible, only to realize that eternity was not a concept of the present, and moments wouldn't last forever. Watching fine strokes forming the irresistible rainbow that attracted our attention no matter what age we were, Cassiopeia realized how delicate moments could be. How fascinating to discover yet another of nature's secrets with the colours of the rainbow always appearing in the same order regardless of where we were...red, orange, yellow, green, blue, indigo, violet.

With a turn of her head she could easily miss the chance to finish making her wish before the rainbow disappeared. Trying to frame moments in order to preserve them for a long time, we often forget to enjoy moments of such serenity while in the midst of them.

Zeus seemed to have changed his set of colours now. Using a darker set of paints, the contrasts were getting stronger and Cassiopeia started to catch the first glimpse of the heavenly bodies which appeared to be of even rarer colours reflecting the remaining light out there before the complete darkness settled in.

Notations

Mana didn't know what to expect. It was a Saturday night and it was a rare occasion that she went out with her parents. They were off to a classical concert performed by the Tokyo Philharmonic Orchestra at the well-known Bunkamura concert hall. Though Mana liked the harmonious and soothing works of art of the world's best-known composers, she wasn't quite sure whether she would be in the mood to enjoy those fine sequences of sounds.

Her mind was with the gemstones. But maybe it was a good combination, her mind's preoccupation with precious thoughts and the delicate pieces of food for her ears.

Being regulars at the Bunkamura concert hall, Mana's parents insisted on her coming along this time as Kazuo Yamada was set to lead. Not giving her the slightest chance to escape, Mana was seated between her parents. The moment the conductor raised his hands, Mana's eyelids surrendered to gravity and closed.

Mana was not asleep but enjoying the intense view in her mind's eye. Imagining an unrefined luminous gemstone in her hand, she was trying to capture the characteristics of the gem which she wanted bring to its full beauty by polishing it. Polishing this luminous treasure to perfection was like using a quill as thin as human hair to write the gem's own story on its surface. In her mind Mana's hand was moving in sync with the waves of the music of the century old Tokyo Philharmonic Orchestra. Line by line she wrote what the gem told her but it was invisible to the human eye, creating a perfectly smooth surface which kept the secret between the one who had found it and held the quill writing it down.

Vast Wideness

Having spent the day at his uncle's place, Tim was full of inspiration. When his parents collected him, he was still daydreaming about what he had seen in his uncle's pictures. He imagined himself as a national park supervisor in Africa. During the day he would follow his duties and monitor the animals' movements and behaviour in his section of the park, occasionally he would assist scientists from all over the world with their research and from time to time he would instruct tourists on correct behaviour in the park. For most of the day, Tim would be outside, and no matter what kept him busy, he would be stunned anew by the vastness of the land in the park. Whether it was dry season or wet season or in between, nature produced miraculous sights every day, which was exactly what filled Tim with a deep sense of satisfaction.

He saw himself sitting in front of his residential tent in one of the park's campsites. It was on top of a hill, with an amazing view over the steppe and some greener areas with watering holes where animals would gather regularly. When the walkie-talkie finally fell asleep and

Tim enjoyed dinner after the entire day outside, he would just sit there and absorb the view. Until the night arrived and blurred the sharp and clear contours of the African vegetation, Tim would gather thoughts and energy for his calling. With a clear sky and no distractions, he would take his notebook that carried marks from the weather conditions and Tim's hands. With his thoughts wandering around he would give in to his aspiration and spend hours writing dreams for others until he fell asleep on his foldable camping chair or was reminded by the active nocturnal animals that it was time to rest. What a privilege it was, having found the perfect surroundings to earn a meaningful living during the day and follow another passion during the night! Lining up word after word in his notebook, Tim hadn't realized that his mum was trying to get him out of the car as she was saying 'Tim, we are home!'

LOST IN TRANSLATION

Why did life feel so difficult? Shouldn't it be easy? Mana had started to see Paolo regularly, but somehow she felt torn. Torn between two different worlds, two cultures, imagination and expectations, rationality and emotions. Something she had wanted for so long was now in reach, yet she didn't know how to deal with it. The warmth, the gentle strokes, the unconditional comfort offered by the special someone, the intimacy - all of it she had imagined, but now that it was tangible she was struggling. Struggling to make sense of it as she had always tried to do in her life, but also struggling to surrender to the uncertainty in life, which promised adventures and moments to treasure but no guarantees. Torn because past memories seemed to hurt, like chains around our limbs. A load that she thought she had shed, but still somehow weighed down on her.

On top of it was her occupational turnaround, which was starting to take shape in front of her inner eyes. A complete change of her life was ahead of her. Gathering the courage to do so was one thing, but dealing with all the new pieces for her personal mosaic was another. Not knowing what the mosaic would look like at the end was challenging, at times driving Mana to despair. She felt lost in translation. Waiting for divine guidance and her own inspiration, Mana reasoned that pursuing one's dreams takes courage and persistence, while learning to love seemed to be a lifelong task.

SHARING THE MOON

It was one of those beautiful warm and long summer nights. Ruth and Walter were sitting on their veranda over a glass of wine, looking at the sky. It was pretty clear after the earlier summer downpour in the afternoon, which barely lasted quarter of an hour and one could nearly watch the raindrops evaporating as they fell since nature was so thirsty.

Ruth and Walter recalled their moments apart when they were young and Walter was often on business trips around the world. No matter where they were, they always left their thoughts for each other with the moon. One would place them there and the other one would collect them. When the moon was full, it almost seemed like a mirror and they imagined seeing each other by looking at that yellowish mirror in the sky. Now they could look at the moon together, holding hands and feeling each other's presence, and they were glad to have discovered this ritual for their relationship. They wondered whether couples in today's constantly connected world still practised seemingly silly stuff, which formed the basis of their lifelong bond.

RIDGE WALK

Enrique was in the United States for training. Over dinner he learnt from the previous participants of the programme what happened after classes were over. The married participants of the foregoing executive programme indulged in affairs while travelling for their studies.

Even when grown up, the fine line of temptation and moral concepts was still a constant ridge walk. Loving freedom, the intertwined responsibility is often forgotten.

How would that change in the near future as our world became transparent in different ways? Would new digital identities accommodate deeply rooted human instincts? Were borders necessary to keep a moral order? Which values were to be cultivated?

IT'S ABOUT TIME!

Cassiopeia was on her way to the international night of the student symposium organized across different faculties. At the entrance to the venue she found eight big round clocks up on the wall, showing the time of major cities across the globe. Waiting with the other students while queuing at the entrance, she kept observing the clocks. Though she was among the vivid discussions of her fellow students, she imagined the sound of the clocks in her head. Tick, tock, tick, tock, tick, tock. All perfectly in sync and without any resistance, the small and big hands moved forward seamlessly. Time was running, a second, a minute, an hour at a time. They all lasted the same across the globe. But what people did or managed to get done within that time was completely different at one side of the globe to the other. Commuting to work in India, walking to the nearest well for a day's clean supply of water in Congo, eating a fast food meal and watching a movie in the United States, getting to the nearest outback hospital in Australia for medical care or attending classes at high school in the UK – all activities that lasted two hours but couldn't be more different. While we are so conscious about how we spend our scarce time on earth we easily forget the relativity of it. Even more so with globalization trying to establish a common pace, we often overlook the variety of concepts of time produced by the socialization of human beings in different cultures. Your turn to enter the venue for the international night Cassiopeia – enjoy your time!

SHORT-SIGHTED BIG FOOT

Back in the office on Friday for the weekly homecoming Marc learnt about the most recent projects his company had acquired. Growth at any cost seemed to be at the top of the charts. One of his junior colleagues informed him about a project to replace a spare parts manufacturing site with sourcing from low-cost countries, consciously compromising on the quality and durability of the goods. Nobody thought about the annoyed customers who would have to replace the spare parts more frequently…because they saved some money as they were cheaper. And the shareholders only had blinking dollar signs in front of their eyes. It seemed to be a luxury of time to think one step ahead and consider the resources and energy required for all the spare parts in the long run. If the quality wasn't the same and durability was compromised, energy and resources were wasted by producing inferior quality products just because it was cheaper. The sole consideration was price or cost. No thoughts were wasted on sustainability, about the lifecycle from the moment the raw materials were extracted until the product retired and was recycled. Interdependencies between people, products and our planet just seemed to be too complex. But that can't be the excuse big foot; we are living at our own expense, or at least at the expense of future generations!

HOLDING THE WORLD IN YOUR HANDS

It was the end of summer and Tim was looking forward to the summer holidays. Today he had his geography class. The teacher would usually share some personal travel experiences since it was the last session before the summer break. This time the teacher went on and on about his recent trip to the Kluane National Park in Canada. He mentioned that this Heritage Site was comprised of huge ice fields, glaciers, Canada's highest peak as well as an abundance of animal species. While he was talking about Canada's vegetation, the enormous Kaskawulah Glacier, snow-capped mountain peaks, encounters with grizzly bears, timber wolves and Canadian lynx, Tim was still paying attention but the moment he turned to the types of trees, camping tips and Dall sheep, his concentration went and he began daydreaming.

If he could hold the globe in his hands, could he just travel the world by turning it and having a closer look? How would it feel? Heavy? Wet? Would his fingers sense the heat of the Sahara Desert or the cold of the Arctic? Would he be able to smell the fresh air in the

Scandinavian pine forests? What would the texture of the world be like? Would he be able to hear the waves of the sea once they were closer to his ear? The smashing sounds of waterfalls? The noise of chaos produced by traffic jams in the middle of Cairo? Tim was tempted to turn it a little quicker than usual or to change the direction of the rotation, not following the Earth's axis. Would the world's citizens become dizzy? Would he disturb the aircraft flying around or the gigantic container ships en route from port to port? He could certainly also hold it still - or would it fall apart? Would the water fall off the globe? What would happen if he shook it in an attempt to wake up all the sleepy humans?

There it was, loud and clear among all the imaginary pictures in his head, the school bell, which meant it was time for Tim to pack up and get ready for the holidays. Too bad he couldn't continue dreaming about holding the world in his hands.

WARMING HEARTS

Mana had another date. She wasn't yet able to put into words what she felt in these moments with Paolo, and maybe she shouldn't attempt to verbalize it anyway. With mixed feelings of excitement and nervousness Mana was getting ready to meet Paolo at the Shinjuku Station. She had been told to come in outdoor wear. Too absorbed in her thoughts and expecting a question from her parents any time about where she was heading, she couldn't imagine where Paolo would be taking her. She could barely think of anything at the moment.

When she finally met him at the station shortly after that, she was surprised to see him carrying a barbecue set, a tiny kettle barbecue to be specific. She caught herself first staring at the grill, then at Paolo. Completely absorbed in her own world she forgot the busy world around her in the midst of the train station. Still wondering where the day would lead, but too shy to say much in this public space, Mana tried to pay full attention to Paolo and at times she thought she caught a glimpse of excitement in his blue eyes. Except for a few words about work, they didn't speak much during the train ride, and Mana didn't want to attract more attention, as she already felt everyone looking at her with this unusual foreign friend. With his nearly black hair Paolo didn't appear to be a typical foreigner at first glance, but it was still obvious that his original home was somewhere else than this part of the world.

Reaching the destination, Paolo revealed his plan for the rest of the day. He wanted to take Mana to one of his favourite spots where she could see the city from afar, while being completely surrounded by nature. For that they would have to hike for about an hour after taking the bus from the station. No wonder he was carrying a well-filled backpack. When Mana asked earlier what she should bring along, Paolo, in his courteous manner, just said 'you will be enough'. Paolo intended to have the barbecue at the viewpoint he had in mind. Mana was stunned. How sweet this was. Such an unusual surprise, she was getting really excited as she had never picnicked like this before. Even less so alone with such a charming man.

With just the two of them on the hiking path Mana tried to be more relaxed, not giving in to her wandering mind but rather paying full attention to the conversation with Paolo. During the course of the hike she learnt that Paolo was the son of a diplomat who moved to Tokyo years ago. When his father was called for his next assignment in another part of the world, Paolo who had then just finished his culinary education as a chef, decided to stay on and try his luck by opening his own business. His parents were a little sceptical but promised their support. Mana was amazed by Paolo's braveness at that age in a foreign land. With her initial tension subsiding, Mana felt an increasing attraction to Paolo and she had an urge to touch him again, to feel the structure of his skin, his warmth like the other day at his place.

Far away from the hustle and bustle of the town, they were now up in the hills with nothing more than peaceful nature surrounding them and a stunning view ahead of them. Wow. Suddenly feelings of romance filled Mana's body. Mana found herself lacking the words to express herself a few times, but Paolo didn't seem to mind, he just enjoyed her presence. Unpacking what he had prepared for the picnic Mana was speechless when she caught sight of all the things he had brought. Her favourite antipasti, which she always had in his shop whenever she dropped by for lunch, carefully marinated and wrapped pieces of meat for their barbecue, lumps of charcoal for the grill, drinks and even a dessert as he had promised.

As Paolo set up the barbecue and the charcoal started to change colour from pitch black to mystical blazing orange-red, Mana felt their hearts warm up. Vivid pictures about the intimate moments they had already spent together filled Mana's mind. Had she already given the key to her heart away?

Everything in Order

Cassiopeia was arranging her lecture notes before the summer break. Working with paper cards for her exam preparation allowed her to cover all the topics systematically.

A heavy summer downpour took her attention away from the notes to the outside. Cassiopeia had this concept in mind about how life was organized. For each human being the creator made a note. On this note the purpose of the new Earth dweller was stated. Everything else was left to chance. The where, how, with whom, when.

It would depend on the Earth dweller when and how quickly their individual path would be discovered. In the studio the creator would keep all the records. Written carefully and sorted day by day, the records were kept. All of them looked the same; there was no distinction according to sex, race or belief. If the Earth dweller lost their way, was discouraged or disappointed the creator retrieved the card. If the Earth dweller didn't have certain capabilities or the required maturity yet, some tasks would be offered again. There was a purpose for all the elements of the clockwork.

Sometimes it was difficult for Earth dwellers, particularly if they had solved all their previous tasks without any problems. But as soon as unexpected tests appeared, they struggled. They grew from it eventually but the process of self-discovery was painful and required lots of energy and courage. However, such challenging tasks would only usually be posed if the Earth dwellers were ready for them.

Often the top-heavy Earth dwellers struggled most with dealing with the realities of life. But even they learnt over time, provided they were willing to adapt their thinking and action patterns and had the courage to go off the beaten track. And usually that started with accepting what life brought with it, without asking why, but instead discovering contradictions and correlations curiously before deciding to act.

The sun was out again and Cassiopeia wanted to finish making her arrangements.

WINDS OF CHANGE

Tim was sitting on the bench where the envelope was discovered a year ago. Though he felt the presence of the others, he enjoyed this moment of solitude as he gazed over the distant valley.

It was autumn. Autumn again. The bi-lobed shaped leaves of the gingko biloba turned golden and lost their vitality slowly. Airily they surrendered to the wind, which took charge of their destinies. The herby taste of autumn filled the air. The gusts of wind were changing from soft to strong, from vigorous to gentle. It was like music to Tim's ears. Sometimes the leaves looked like planes taking off. However, they did not try to control their journey but left it to chance where the gust took them next.

Cassiopeia joined Tim and watched nature's periodic spectacle silently. Leaves grew from strong scions, prospered into dark green photosynthesis factories and then said farewell after completing their job. Even if the leaves sometimes appeared to defend themselves and did not want to let go of the tree, they continued their journey sooner or later. Coming and going was natural. Almost like the thoughts of an experienced meditating monk, who welcomed all his thoughts and allowed them to move on without holding on to them tightly. In the flow of change, with the power of the wind.

Japan

Mana struggled to change her profession completely, especially because of the social expectations that she was used to fulfilling. She still caught herself frequently acting according to those patterns, which she had followed throughout her upbringing. It was extremely challenging to direct them in a new way. Often discouraged, Mana liked to recall the wise words of one of her friends who once said, taking small steps, we run long distances. So, step by step Mana.

Mana's relationship with Paolo had intensified, although there were occasionally difficult moments, particularly when Mana was in doubt about herself and her place in the world. She was grateful that Paolo had an extremely big heart and loved her unconditionally. Mana even had the courage to introduce Paolo to her parents. A little surprised, they were happy to see that Mana had found her soul mate. Rather traditional in their thinking, they didn't comment much but Mana saw that they weren't used to having a foreigner in their family. But over time things fell into place and Paolo was warmly received within her family.

***

Two years on Mana and Paolo had the indescribable joy to inform their parents that they would be grandparents soon. They had decided to get married just months earlier after Paolo proposed to Mana during a stay in a traditional Ryokan at the foot of Mount Fuji. Paolo insisted on a completely traditional wedding in Japan but they also wanted to have a ceremony in Italy in order to reunite their family members from all over the world to celebrate their special day.

***

Since Mana's decision to change her professional path had grown firmer, she started to take small steps towards realizing her dream of becoming a gem hunter. She started by joining the local crystallography association to learn more about the secrets of the trade, she connected with others with similar interests and even got in touch with professionals around the globe by joining some exhibitions for which she took leave from her current job. At the beginning she did it all in secret, only Paolo was aware of her plans. Over time she started revealing some of her ideas to her parents who were surprised to know that Mana had suddenly changed direction. Most likely because they themselves had never had a chance to follow their own calling. When they grew up, there wasn't much opportunity for self-realization, as funds were limited and securing an income was the highest priority. Countless options were not available so there was no confusion about which to choose, but they were created by the innovative thinkers of their generation through hard work. Now, the world was a different one, yet the quest for happiness continued and the succeeding generations struggled to make sense of the world. What are we here for if choice is unlimited; the traditional working models no longer satisfy the urge for a work-life balance, fulfilment, professional challenges and an enriching private life? These were questions that returned to Mana randomly.

***

Encouraged and supported by Paolo, Mana slowly but surely intensified her exchange with other gem hunters around the globe. She learnt more about the requirements of such a profession and started to consider further education to acquire the necessary qualifications. While attending a gathering of the Japanese crystallography association, Mana took a break at the coffee corner as she was a little exhausted from all the impressions she had gathered while walking through the exhibition and listening attentively to the different speeches. As she sipped her iced mocha and stared out into the blue absorbed in thought, an old gentleman asked her permission to join her at the table. Though enjoying the moments of solitude, she somehow didn't mind his company as he reminded her of her grandfather who was a wise man, who always found the right words to comfort her when she seemed to have lost touch with the ground as her thoughts carried her away. Briefly glancing at each other a few times, Mana hesitated to initiate a conversation. She didn't know where or what to start with. And her counterpart still seemed to be trying to make sense of this young, beautiful but apparently shy lady at such an occasion. Unable to bear the silence any longer Mana tried to form a question in her mind. Only when she noticed that the old man was staring at her with complete incomprehension did she realize that she hadn't said anything out loud which was in her mind. She blushed and immediately felt uncomfortable, but the soothing calm voice of the unknown vis-à-vis encouraged her to try one more time. Somehow she gathered the courage and with a little more confidence she asked the gentleman what his name was and what had brought him to this event. Slightly taken aback by this young lady's direct question, but yet, somehow positively surprised, the gentleman explained that he was a retired gem trader in the Kyoto area and now lived in Takashima in a quiet spot overlooking Lake Biwa. He had retired nearly 10 years ago but his wife encouraged him to stay in touch with his old colleagues and friends around the globe in this rather rare trade, which had been an integral part of his life for decades. The tension subsided as Mana grew somehow more comfortable sitting opposite this stranger who seemed to share a similar interest. Enquiring about her profession, Mana was first reluctant to reveal much about herself, but then guided by an invisible force she nevertheless decided to share part of the story of her life, particularly her career as an accountant during which suddenly realized that gem stones were far closer to her heart than figures. Kusagawa, which was the gentleman's name as Mana learnt later on, was overwhelmed by the unexpected twist in Mana's story. She seemed to long for encouragement, for some visionary input that would foster her thinking and decision process. When he enquired about her future plans Mana confirmed Kusagawa's initial perception - she didn't know how to take the next step. Kusagawa remained quiet and took a sip of his coffee. Mana wasn't quite sure whether she should leave or stay, remain quiet or try to revive the conversation. She had rarely had such encounters with strangers in the last few years and had only grown a little more accustomed to enjoying such moments since she met Paolo. When the silence nearly became unbearable, Kusagawa took out a small notebook with a fine pearl-coloured washi paper cover from the inner pocket of his jacket. He flipped through the notebook until he found the first blank page and firmly wrote something in Japanese. He carefully tore the page out of the notebook and handed it to Mana without any comment. Bowing her head in appreciation and receiving the piece of paper with both hands, Mana recognized that the neat handwriting stated a name and a phone number. Mana stared at Kusagawa in disbelief as he rose from the chair and was about to leave. Kusagawa said, 'call the man on the paper, tell him your story and I am sure he will invite you to join him on one of his next business trips to Myanmar'. Astonished and with her mouth open, Mana watched Kusagawa making his way through the crowd.

***

After the gathering, Mana met Paolo. She was still baffled by the events of the day and was really excited to see Paolo. They met at their favourite traditional Japanese sushi restaurant in the neighbourhood of her parents' place. It was a small family run restaurant, which just had eight seats and a small bar with some additional seats. The food was excellent and skilfully prepared by the chef who came up with seasonal creations daily. It was a little chilly as Mana waited outside the restaurant for Paolo to arrive but luckily she didn't have to wait long. Paolo just turned around the corner with his old imported Italian racing bike, which he parked and locked to the nearest street lamp. He embraced Mana warmly and kissed her as if they were at home and Mana blushed instantly. Although she enjoyed the sensation of Paolo's lips and tongue, she wasn't used to such open displays of affection. Paolo saw that Mana was holding back some news but suggested they take their seats in the restaurant first. The daughter of the restaurant owner welcomed them back, and as regulars they had their favourite table. Sitting down on the tatami mats, they were provided with the handwritten menu of the day. After a quick glance at the beautifully written Japanese characters, which were still a miracle to Paolo, they decided to go for the chef's recommendation. And then Mana burst like a bubble. Overcome by excitement, she swallowed half of her words as she spoke too quickly.

***

Over time, Mana learnt to ride the waves of the river of life instead of fearing them. While she had always been frightened by the uncertainty that life brought with it, she slowly learnt step-by-step how to deal with it. The relationship with Paolo gave her the necessary strength to treat unexpected moments as opportunities instead of challenges. She started to enjoy a different quality of life, which was more real and more intense. It took time and patience for her to learn how to deal with these new sensations, but with so many dreams in mind she was determined to make the best out of her life. She appreciated every day without worrying unnecessarily. Fleeing and running away was no longer an option. Instead, Mana learnt how to face uncertainty and gained enormous strength from doing so. Avoidance was no longer the strategy for growing. With every step she took she gained more confidence, training a new muscle in her body.

SWITZERLAND

Cassiopeia was progressing well in her studies. She enjoyed the input that she got for her philosophical discourses, which always brought her a step closer to understanding how the world ticked from her point of view. She even had the chance to take on a part time job as an assistant at the neuroscience faculty, a perfect fit to cultivate her interest in this domain.

Helping out occasionally at the paper and print shop in town and joining yoga classes at a newly opened centre made her feel content with her current life – with no urge for more.

UNITED KINGDOM

Marc was in tears, fearing he was nearing a nervous breakdown, he didn't know how to stem what was expected from him at work. Producing meaningless reports with instructions on how to manipulate them for the decision makers was just too much for his conscience. It seemed to be the last straw. Not knowing where to head next, he had always decided to stay put in his current job. But now he was being forced to rethink his way forward. He didn't want to end like other stars of the economy.

Realizing his desperate situation, Marc's colleagues encouraged him to take an extended unpaid holiday. It wouldn't just give him a break from all the daily chores of his consultant life but would also create an opportunity for relaxation, distraction and new thoughts, which were suffocated as long as he tried to cope with the increasing workload and dissatisfaction. Also, it would allow him to spend time with Laura, to find out whether they were meant for each other or whether it was time to part. Determined to ask for a break, Marc requested an appointment with his boss for the next office day, which was at end of the week. He knew his boss was never in favour of quick decision-making but he hoped he would realize the seriousness of Marc's condition.

***

Marc's boss surprisingly agreed to Marc's proposal. He spent his sabbatical connecting with different people, attending exhibitions on his areas of interest and intense moments of togetherness with Laura. He also got in touch with various NGOs and upon his return to work he had gained clarity about his priorities in life. This was consulting as long as it satisfied him but no longer as a 200% job, more quality time with his friends and Laura, regular sports and some meaningful volunteer engagement during his spare time.

***

Returning to work was more challenging than Marc had expected. He easily lost his motivation and was often discouraged by the smallest incident. One day on his way to work Marc received an unexpected call from one of his ex-study mates. He knew little about the firm that his friend worked with, but apparently it was a boutique consultancy, which took a different approach to enabling firms to achieve their goals. Unaware of this hidden pearl, Marc felt the first moments of excitement he had felt for a long time. His mind immediately started picturing himself working closely with his ex-study mate. It could even be a stepping-stone for his own business at a later stage.

***

Marc decided to join the boutique consultancy after a short moment of consideration. He usually didn't decide lightly on such matters but felt it was the right thing to do. With all he had learnt about the firm during a few discussions, he was convinced he would find a more promising environment for his future development and also a better work-life balance.

This was what Marc was longing for as he didn't want to jeopardize his relationship with Laura any further. The moment he had made his decision to move on, a warm feeling of satisfaction and sparks of new energy and motivation started to rise from his toes, to his feet, slowly filling his entire body. This was a feeling that was almost foreign to him as he hadn't experienced such a mood for months. Suddenly he was full of enthusiasm to change his life, doing sports regularly, enjoying cultural events with Laura, growing his own vegetables in his garden, and spending some time doing volunteer activities. Pleased about the events of the day, Marc sank into a deep and relaxing sleep.

Finally, he had found continuity within himself and not in the ever-changing environment.

SWITZERLAND

Tim was more determined than ever to pursue his dreams no matter what others said. He was convinced that the world would be a better place if people listened to their hearts and followed their dreams, even though economists tried to build rational models around the behaviour of the homo economicus.

***

School filled most of Tim's schedule but besides that he continued to work on his different ventures. He wrote numerous dreams for Clara, though he didn't succeed easily. Clara frequently complained that she didn't dream what Tim had written and Tim was unsure why his dream-writing did not work as expected. Yet, he felt, it was too early to give up and maybe he should refine his works.

***

After completing his current term, Tim was invited by his uncle to join him on his next trip to Africa. Feeling excitement in each and every fibre of his body, Tim spent his spare hours in the community library looking at photography and documentary books about Namibia, particularly books about the Etosha national park, where they would be going in a few weeks.

Spain

Holding on dearly to his principles and values, Enrique became more confident in dealing with temptations as he realized they were always part of our lives, even if we learnt how to deal with them differently. Sometimes they were just the right spice to keep life prickling.

***

Enrique continued to travel extensively for his job but started to make a point of being in the office regularly since he loved the infrequent encounters with Luz. He slowly started to feel comfortable revealing more about himself, what bugged him, what excited him, what he looked forward to. So did Luz.
For Enrique those moments weren't just other temptations, they were rooted more deeply and just felt right. Though still a novelty to him, he learnt to appreciate this form of togetherness.

***

As with their first chat in the office months ago, Luz was always good for a surprise. One day, while out for lunch with Luz, Enrique was taken aback when she asked him to join a dancing class with her. He couldn't say no – the attraction was overwhelming. And so they started dancing, becoming closer step-by-step…

Germany

Having their usual glass of wine on their terrace, Ruth and Walter were happy. No longer living at home since Walter's stroke, they had now found a comfortable place and the necessary care facilities in a new type of community for retirees.

As age progressed relentlessly, they were glad to see subtle positive changes in society. There was still a long way to go, but at last there were change makers starting with good initiatives, going back to basics, back to more reasonable ways of living sustainably, appreciating produce, and maintaining close relationships with the farmers who grow our food. Kids could be kids again, as scientists and parents finally realized that constant tuition did not produce content kids in the long run.

Not a bad outlook for the twilight years.

In Motion

At one point in history mankind was scared of the steaming beast and scientists claimed that humans couldn't take the pace of those vehicles. Yet we know that we are wired for motion. It unlocks the flow of our thoughts and when motion takes control over consciousness, unconsciousness could work.

I was in motion when most of what you have read was created. I was on a train, driving, taking a flight, jogging or going for a walk. Only when I paused, or the world was asleep, did I manage to put into words what you have just finished reading.

We don't necessarily see less when we stay put in one location, but as everything evolves around us, flow has a different intensity and depth.

Namasté.